Dark
PROTECTOR
BLACK HOODS MC# 1

D1714345

Dark Protector © 2020 Avelyn Paige & Geri Glenn

Dark Protector

Blair's life isn't perfect, but she has a plan. Find a new roommate, finish school and finally start the future she's been working so hard for.

And then he knocks on her door. One unwanted visitor is all it took to crush her reality and leave her living in fear. But at least she's living, thanks to the help of a good Samaritan.

A very sexy, tattooed and motorcycle-riding man with a dog that looks as savage as he is sweet. Green-Peace saves her. He makes her feel safe. He makes her feel a lot of things she's never felt before.

But, the danger's not over. Her attacker is still there, lurking in the shadows and waiting to strike again. GreenPeace will put his life and his club on the line to save the captivating woman that's stolen his heart. But even that might not be enough.

To the pebble of doom.
Thanks for not screwing up our deadline.

Chapter 1

BLAIR

"THIS IS IT," I declare to the young, dark-haired woman behind me. "Home sweet home. Feel free to take a look around."

She steps into the entryway, and her eyes immediately gaze up at the ornate wooden design on the ceiling —one of my favorite features of the house. There are a lot of older homes on this block, but my house is the prettiest, most original of them all, thanks to grandmother's creative mind and grandfather's carpentry skills.

"Wow," she murmurs, glancing down at one of the flyers I'd posted all around campus over the last few weeks. "I was expecting a shit hole for this price, but this place is actually pretty decent. A little old and musty, but not bad."

Strike one. I grit my teeth and try to smile, but it's

taking every ounce of manners I have to keep a straight face. Grandmother taught me to never make rash decisions based on a first impression, but I can already tell this woman's not the kind of roommate I'm looking for. Just as I think this, Jinx hisses from the landing upstairs.

"I don't like cats," she scowls, looking in Jinx's direction. "Is he always inside?"

"She's a *girl*," I answer flatly. If I let this woman stay here, Jinx would leave furball gifts in all her shoes, and dead mice in her bed. "And yes, she's an indoor cat."

"I see," she huffs.

From creepy guys to foreign students who didn't speak a single word of English, the entire process of finding new tenants has been nothing short of a nightmare. Why in the hell did my best friends have to graduate early? The better question might be, why did I pick a program that required graduate school to be licensed? After nearly three weeks of showings, and no reasonable person to fill a vacancy, I'm really starting to question a lot of things in my life.

Is it me? Am I the problem?

"The kitchen is just through there." I motion toward the hallway, just off the entry. "There's a bathroom on this floor, and another on the second where the bedrooms are. Laundry is in the basement."

She continues to take in the vintage fixtures as she quietly moves to the living room. The heels of her boots clack loudly on the hardwood, the sound setting my teeth on edge. She stops near the leather L-shaped couch before turning back to me with a look of pure confusion on her face. "So, what's the catch?"

Stunned, I open my mouth to respond with something snarky, and then snap it shut, questioning instead with, "Excuse me? I don't know what you mean by that," as I take a few long strides to close the distance between us.

Rolling her eyes, she crosses her arms over her chest. "You heard me. What's the catch?"

"There's no catch," I say, trying to keep my tone even. "What you see is what you get."

Honestly, she isn't the first person to ask about my ad. The same ad I'd read through at least half a dozen times before posting it. The pictures alone should've given any potential renter a good idea of what they were getting. It's not like I found random photos of a house on Google and slapped them onto the ad.

I'm learning that cheap rent is a red flag for such a nice house, especially in a neighborhood so close to campus. I could count on two hands the offers I've turned down over the years from both the university and local developers. This shouldn't be rocket science. Nice house. Good rent. Non-psychotic roommate. Okay cat. If the roles were reversed, I'd have jumped at the opportunity.

"Yeah, right," she fires back, her eyebrows arched in disbelief. "Where's the rug you're going to pull out from under me? Because this place is far too nice for what you're asking. Did someone die here?"

Strike two. You're about one comment away from being struck from the list altogether, lady.

"The house is in perfect working order, if that's what you're implying. And no, it's not a murder house. I just need a roommate to help with bills over the summer session. I already have a roommate lined up for the fall semester."

Thank God for that. I just wish Melissa had decided to stay for the summer and take extra classes instead of leaving me in a bind, but I understand why she did it. After almost not graduating, she needed a break. Especially with the rigorous program we were about to step into this fall with a full schedule of graduate school and teaching assistant requirements.

The girl huffs silently under her breath. *You try to help someone out, and this is the response you get.* Her persistence in trying to find faults with the house only makes my decision easier. She's not what I'm looking for, no matter how desperate I am for help with the monthly bills. There must be a better way to keep my late grandmother's 1917 Victorian home. I'm starting to deeply regret turning down the last girl who came to see the house. Sure, she had a dog, and Jinx would lose her shit, but her attitude was way better than this chick's.

"Are you a psycho or something? Is that why this place hasn't been snatched up?"

Strike three. I can deal with her shitty attitude, but calling me a psycho within minutes of stepping foot into my home? Not happening. There are four more people waiting in the wings to come look at this house. At this point, they would have to be complete whack jobs in order for me to breathe the same air as this woman on a daily basis.

"I think we're done here," I clip out. "You and me," —I motion between us— "are just not going to work."

"No, wait," she cries, her hands going up in surrender. "I didn't mean to come off as a bitch. I'm sorry. I'm just... I'm not good at the whole 'people' thing. This place is really great, and I'd love to be your roommate."

"I'm sorry, but you've insulted me, my home, and my cat. You can't seriously think I would consider having you move in here. You need to leave. Now."

"Please, give me another chance," she begs, her nasty, arrogant attitude gone. "I can't afford anything else this close to campus, and I'm on a really tight budget. My student loans haven't been approved yet, and I start class next week. I really need this."

As much as I sympathize with her story, I need to take care of myself first. I know giving this chick a place to live will do serious damage to my mental health. "I'm sorry, but it's a no from me."

"You've got to be kidding me!" she whines, stomping her foot in a tantrum worthy of a preschooler. "I said I was sorry."

"And I asked you to leave, but your feet don't seem to be moving any closer to the door. Let me remind you where it is." Walking back to the entry, I open the door wide, directing her with my hand to take the hint. She has fifteen seconds at the most before I forcibly remove her or call campus police.

The woman fumes as she storms out past me, spluttering a string of curses that would make a sailor blush, as she stomps down the walkway to the sidewalk.

I step out onto the porch, watching to make sure she's gone before closing the door behind me. Sighing heavily, I head to the kitchen to warm up the leftovers from last night's dinner. *And, she called me the psycho.* She's in desperate need of professional help, the kind that I—in three more years—can give her. Well, that is, if I survive them. Grabbing a bowl out of the refrigerator, I pop off the lid and shove it in the microwave. The second the first button beeps, a familiar *meow* calls from behind.

"It's not dinnertime yet, Jinx." She meows back, but this time with a little more attitude behind it. "Don't you sass me like that."

She jumps on the counter next to me, the one place

she knows she's not supposed to be. But cats are notorious for making up their own rules.

"What do you think you're doing, little girl?" The second I reach out to grab her, she flops onto her belly, doing her *I'm a cute little kitty* dance. I finally get my hands around her black, furry middle, and help her back down to the kitchen floor, just in time for the microwave to beep.

I head back toward the living room and plop down onto the couch with my dinner and Jinx in tow. It's actually nice that showing ended early—despite the unpleasantness of the prospective renter—because it's been weeks since I've gotten to eat sitting down instead of grabbing a bowl of whatever leftovers are in the fridge and eating on the walk to class.

Grabbing the remote, I click on a Netflix show I've been dying to start while shoveling a bite of macaroni and cheese into my mouth. It's not until I go to take a second bite that Jinx, who's perched on the back of the couch, tries to pull the bowl away from me.

"Jinx!" I snap. Bouncing off the couch, she runs off to the entryway and bolts up the stairs to her angry kitty dome. It's her bat cave of solitude when she gets scolded. The sheer brazenness of her actions shouldn't really surprise me, but after three and a half years of cohabitating together, there's not much the little black furball of mischief won't try at least once.

After scarfing down my food, I head into the kitchen to clean up my bowl, just as the doorbell rings.

"Huh." I glance at the clock on the microwave. "She's early." Maybe that's a good sign. *Early might mean eager.* Whoever she is, she has to be worlds better than the last one. Drying my hands off with a towel, I make my way to the door.

Jinx meows down at me. "Oh, hush up," I warn her, taking a quick second to straighten up my clothes before flinging open the door for my next potential renter.

"Hello…" I greet cheerfully, but I don't even get a chance to finish the sentence. The person standing on my porch isn't the post-graduate student I'd been expecting. Instead, it's my worst nightmare.

A hooded figure, clad in dark jeans and a black hoodie, stands in my doorway, a knife gleaming in their hand. A stranger with clear, dubious intentions. With one flash of the weapon under the porch light, my entire world slows down to a snail's pace.

I try to scream, to shut the door, but the intruder blocks it with a large, gloved hand. My feet falter underneath me, causing me to play into the intruder's plan. Grabbing me by the hair, they drag me closer to the danger zone. With undeniable fear coursing through every inch of my veins, my body freezes.

The man, I believe, based on their build, presses the

knife under my chin. When a heavy blow lands to the side of my head, everything goes black.

One final thought crosses my mind as I lose consciousness.

I'm going to die.

Chapter 2

GREENPEACE

"DO you have to piss on every single fucking tree we pass?" I groan as Walter lifts his leg for the hundredth time in less than twenty minutes.

Walter hears me, but he doesn't give a shit. He knows I'll stop when he does, and when a dog's gotta go, a dog's gotta go.

We have an understanding, Walter and me. I treat him with respect, and take him for his hour-long walk each night, allowing him to scout out the neighborhood. In turn, he gives me unconditional love, and doesn't tear my house up. It's a win-win for both of us, especially for him.

Walter's history is dark and twisted, and he's lucky to be alive. Our journey together started when my club busted up a vicious dog fighting ring. I found him lying in a rusty cage, torn and bloodied, waiting to die. With one look from his lone brown eye, I knew he needed me. And maybe, I'd needed him too. So, as much as I might complain about Walter's love of watering the neighborhood, he can piss on as many goddamn trees as he wants to.

Just as Walter is finishing up, some chick storms toward me, her phone plastered to the side of her face while swearing like a trucker to someone on the other end. "Yes!" she snaps. "The dumb bitch kicked me out for no reason!"

I jump to the side to avoid her slamming into me. "Don't mind me," I call out to her back. *Stupid bitch.*

She whirls around to tell me off, but as soon as her eyes land on Walter, they widen, and she mutters a sad excuse for an apology before going on her way.

"Women," I huff, and then chuckle when Walter chuffs in agreement.

Walter turns the corner without prompting, our nightly route embedded in him just as much as it is me. I used to try to detour, to walk other routes, but he's a creature of habit. He doesn't deviate from routine, and he'll be damned if I ever attempt to change it.

The street's quiet, as usual, with Victorian homes lining the road. Great oak trees and maples fill the front yards, their branches reaching toward the sky, providing a privacy other neighborhoods don't possess.

I've always loved this area of town. It's quiet, elegant,

and filled with a history that has always intrigued me. Grandmother had lived here her entire life. When we lost her, and she left her house to me, moving in was a no-brainer. This place is more of a home to me than my childhood one had ever been. It just needed a lot of work after years of neglect.

Walter nearly yanks my arm out of its socket, pulling me from my thoughts.

"Walter!" I snap, tugging lightly on the leash.

He yanks harder, his body reaching and stretching toward one of the houses.

"Walter!" I call again, giving another tug to get his attention.

His head comes around so he can glance back at me, his body still straining against the leash. To some people, he must appear terrifying, but when I look at him, all I see is intelligence and loyalty.

The dog fighting had left the giant, white American Bulldog scarred. His lip had been torn. One of his eyes was missing. His left ear was ripped clean off, and his fur didn't grow over the scars crisscrossing his face and body. But right now, I don't see the scars. I see determination, and an attempt to tell me something.

"Come on, buddy," I try again. "Let's get a move on."

This time, Walter doesn't just strain for the house. This time, he's desperate. An agonized whine rips from his throat, and his nails scrape against the pavement.

That's when I hear it. A short, muffled scream, followed by the sound of something shattering.

Walter's leash yanks from my hand as I stare up at the house. Before I can stop him, he's running for the door.

I know this place. This is the redhead's house. The gorgeous redhead I look for every time we pass, hoping like hell she'll be on her porch doing yoga again. I don't know who invented yoga pants, but I thank fuck they did. They cover that tight little ass of hers like a second skin. Not that I've looked… much.

"Walter, get back here!" I order, rushing to catch him, but he's already at the door, which is ajar. *This is wrong.*

Walter disappears inside, a deep growl ripping from his chest. My feet hit the front porch, and that growl turns to a blood chilling snarl.

Rushing inside, my heart sinks. The redhead is curled in the fetal position on the floor, unconscious, a pool of blood surrounding her head. Just a few feet away, a man's sprawled out on the floor, a mask covering his face, his arm firmly held in Walter's jaws. With a large knife clutched in that hand, he uses the other to punch at my dog.

"You motherfucker!" I roar, jumping over the girl, ready to lay a smackdown on the son of a bitch.

"Please," he cries, pain clear in his voice. "Please, call off your dog. He's hurting me."

With blood dripping down his jowls, Walter shakes the man's arm, pulling him deeper into the house.

Instead of intervening, I reach forward, pluck the knife from the man's hand, and toss it out of his reach. Now that's he's without his weapon, I rear back my foot and land a blow to the side of his head, knocking him out cold.

Walter releases him and moves to the girl. I kneel down to make sure the guy's truly out before turning my back on him. I need to check on the redhead, but what I don't need is a knife in my back.

Yep. He's out.

Spinning around, I shove Walter aside and reach for her. She's breathing, but it's shallow. And if the gash on her right temple tells me anything, it's that she needs medical attention, now.

"Fuck," I mutter, yanking my phone from my pocket. The last thing I need is any sort of attention from the police. The Black Hoods are in the middle of something big at the moment, and me getting mixed up in this could be the end of all our hard work.

"Nine-one-one, what's your emergency? Do you need police, fire, or ambulance?"

"Ambulance, now!" I snap, my mind racing over how to handle this. "And police." Jumping up, I run out to the front porch and give her the address. "A woman's been attacked. She's unconscious and bleeding."

The dispatcher begins her barrage of questions, but I don't wait to hear them. It's bad enough they now have my number on record as placing the call, but I don't want to be here when the police show up. I can't be here, not with the patch on my back. My club isn't exactly friendly with LEOs.

Back inside the house, Walter stands over the woman, pushing and prodding at her face with his nose as he whines in distress. Remembering the man had a knife, I kneel down beside her once more, doing my best to check for stab wounds without disturbing her.

I look down the hall behind me. He's gone. The motherfucker who attacked her must've slipped out the back door when I was outside. *Do I go after him?*

The girl on the floor moans, her head turning from side to side. *Fuck. Guess that answers that.*

"It's okay," I tell her, taking her tiny hand in mine. "You're safe now."

Her green eyes flutter open, barely focusing on me before drifting closed once more.

I can't leave her now. That cowardly fuck can wait, but I will find him. Walter did some damage to his arm, so he's going to need medical attention himself. When he goes to get it, I'll be waiting, coiled like a viper, ready to strike when he least expects it.

BLAIR

THEY SAY your life flashes before your eyes in situations like this, but I can tell you for a fact, that's utter bullshit. I didn't see my life like a movie reel projecting in front of me. I saw the cold, dark eyes of the person about to take my life staring back at me from my own front porch. I could feel the evil oozing from his every pore when he rushed toward me, pressing his knife under my chin.

The rest was a complete blur. Jinx hissing. Pain. Growling. Screams from my attacker. Darkness. Except, there was one moment when I thought I heard a man talking to me. A peaceful presence in the swirling chaos of the attack until darkness swallowed me down into unconsciousness. He had to be a figment of my imagination. I don't know anyone around here with my roommates now gone.

Why would there suddenly be a man riding to my rescue like a knight on a white horse? That didn't happen in real life, and this sure as shit isn't a fairy tale.

The muffled voices of people talking stir me from the abyss, but the pain is nearly unbearable. My head aches like it went a round with a freight train and lost. I try to speak, but only a groan escapes my lips. A consolation prize for still being alive, though barely, if my pain level were the only thing in play. My entire body aches, but my head's the worst of it.

"Miss Thompson, can you hear me?" a female's voice calls out to me through the fog.

I desperately want to answer, but a cascade of warmth flairs to life in my veins. Sweet relief comes soon after, calming the drum-like beats inside my skull. They've given me something for the pain, or a mallet to the head. It doesn't matter, as either option would be suitable at this point.

"What do we have?" a gruff male voice questions.

A dozen pair of hands shift, poking and prodding me while I try to force myself to wake. *Come on, eyes. Just open.* The pleading clearly doesn't do a damn thing to wake me. The pain medicine is doing its job a little too well.

The woman's voice reports the information. It would be hypnotic if not for the fact that I'd just been attacked.

"Female, early twenties, attacked in her home. Defensive wounds on her hands and arms, and a laceration over her right eye. Blood pressure is slightly elevated, but other vital signs are normal. Patient was unconscious when paramedics arrived on the scene."

"Let's get an X-ray of her abdomen and chest, and a CT scan. Sedate her until we can fully assess her injuries."

"Yes, Dr. Malic," is the last thing the woman says before I succumb to the darkness once more.

———

When the fog lifts enough that I can finally open my eyes, it seems like hours have passed. The stark white walls of a hospital room gleam back at me under the early morning sun. *Sunrise? How long have I been out?* I try to shift in the bed, but the IV in my arm tugs, setting off an alarm in the process. The beeping only serves to intensify the pounding in my head.

"Someone's awake, I see," a cheerful nurse says as she walks into the room with a fresh IV bag in her hand. Switching out the bag, she then walks over to the computer terminal next to it. "How's your pain? Scale of one to ten."

"Six," I reply. My throat strains to get out that single word. "Water?"

"The doctor hasn't cleared you for anything to drink

or eat yet," she explains. "I just sent off a note to your attending physician that you're awake. I suspect he'll be in to see you shortly. We'll see if we can get that NPO order lifted."

The nurse flitters out the door, leaving me to my own devices. Every movement I make results in a jolt of pain radiating all over my body, like an electrical current hopping from one limb to the next. No matter how I shift myself, I can't find any semblance of comfort.

Finding the remote attached to the bed, I press the call button for the nurse's station. I need something for the pain, and now. Heavy footsteps come from the hallway, and then a tall doctor steps into the room with a clipboard in his hands, distracting me momentarily from my discomfort.

"It's good to see you awake, Miss Thompson. I'm Dr. Malic. We met earlier, but I doubt you remember much of your arrival." He smiles at me. *Funny guy. Great. Exactly the opposite kind of doctor I need right now.* He steps closer to my bedside, retrieves a flashlight from his pocket, and shines it into my eyes.

"Pupil reflexes are responsive," he mutters, clicking his flashlight off and depositing it back into his pocket. "Your CT scan and X-rays were clear. You do have a mild concussion, and a small laceration we stitched up above your right eye. All things considered, Miss Thompson, you're very lucky."

I don't think I'd call being attacked lucky, but he's right. I could be dead. There's always an upside to everything, I guess.

"I'd like to keep you here for another day, just to err on the side of caution." He nods, disappearing only a few seconds later without so much as a goodbye.

Another day here? Under normal circumstances, I would be fine with that, except for Jinx. I have no way of knowing whether or not she's okay. The thought of her being hurt and alone unsettles me, because she has no one but me to care for her. I can't stay here for another night, at least for her sake. Even if the idea of stepping foot back into my house—which will never quite feel the same again—alone so soon after the attack, scares the holy hell out of me. One way or another, I'm breaking out of this place, even if I have to leave against medical advice.

The nurse returns with a white paper cup, along with a plastic carafe of water, taking my attention away from the painful memories filling my head. She hands me a cup of water and two white pills that go down like lead balloons against sandpaper as I swallow them. Taking another sip of water, it burns slightly less than it did the first time. The nurse takes the cup and sets it on the bedside table.

"Would you like to sit up?"

I nod, and she reaches for the remote to lift the head of my bed.

"You've got quite the entourage out in the waiting room," she informs me with a teasing smile.

I frown. "Excuse me?" *Why would I have an entourage?* It's not like I know anyone close by, and all my neighbors are gone for the summer. The nurse shifts to the other side of the bed and re-adjusts the pillow behind my head.

"The guy that came in with you—the one with all the leather and the dog? He's been out in the waiting room all night. Made quite the scene when they wouldn't let him back to see you without showing his ID. The dog nearly bit one of the security guards."

Dog? I shoot her a look of confusion. I was alone, so she must be mistaken. I have no one close by—not a soul. I'd call my parents, but I doubt they'd even care. The second I moved in with my grandmother at fifteen, I was no longer their problem. They didn't even show up for her funeral three years ago. They did, however, contact her attorney to see if she'd left them anything in her will.

"It's not like you could miss him, or the half dozen of his friends dressed just like him that showed up a few hours after you did. They've been sitting out there ever since. Must be nice to have that many cute guys around, huh?"

"I didn't come here with anyone." Seriously. If I had a

man in my life, I'd more than likely not be in the situation I currently find myself in.

"I get it. I wouldn't want to share either." She winks as she tucks the blanket tightly around my feet, eliciting a hiss from me. "You might want to talk to him about that dog, though. A hospital's no place for an animal like that."

What dog? I don't have a dog. Who the hell is this guy? There wasn't anyone else there but Jinx and me. Unless…

No. It can't be.

Was the voice I heard comforting me real after all?

Chapter 4

GREENPEACE

"SO, you never saw this fucker's face at all?" Karma asks after I finish explaining my story to the rest of the guys.

Sighing, I drag a hand over my face, exhausted after the massive surge of adrenaline I experienced earlier, and anxious to know what exactly is going on down the hall with Blair. "No. Dude had on a balaclava, and I never got a chance to take it off."

"Looks like Walter got a good chunk out of him, though," Judge notes, pointing a finger at the sleeping dog, his muzzle stained with dried blood from the mystery fucknut's arm.

The nurse nearly had a coronary when I burst into the emergency room with Walter at my side, but one look from me, she shut her mouth pretty damn quick. He and I had just been through something intense, and there was no way in hell I was stopping to take him home before I went to the hospital. Besides, all I'd done was kick the fucker. It was Walter who had rushed in and saved the redhead. I hadn't even known her real name until the medic had gone into her purse by the front door and searched out her ID.

"He got him good," I confirm. "I gave him a decent boot to the head, too, so my guess is he's also got a wicked concussion right now. He'll need a doctor, and when he goes to one, we need to be there."

Judge nods, chewing on his lip. "There are only four hospitals within a two-hour drive of here. I'll send a couple of guys to each one, and when he shows up, we'll nail him."

And this is why I called him. Judge may be the president of the club, but he's a brother first. He's one of the scariest sons of bitches I've ever met, but he'd give the shirt off his back for any one of us. And when it comes to someone committing violence against another person who can't defend themselves, he sees red.

I don't know who that fucker was, or why he was in Blair's house, but the fact that he had the foresight to wear a mask tells me she'll likely not have a clue who he is either. He attacked her in her own home, and if it hadn't been for Walter, who knows what would've happened to her.

The memory of her lying on the floor, her gorgeous

red hair stained crimson with her own blood, makes me wish I could turn back the clock and kill the bastard when I had the chance. But ensuring she was all right had been the most important thing to me at the time.

"We're going to find him," Judge says, clapping a hand on my shoulder with a firm squeeze.

Nodding, I stand a little straighter when a doctor enters the waiting room. Hospital policy states you must be an immediate family member to accompany the patient into the treatment area. And even though I'd lied and said I was her fiancé, there was no way they were letting me back there. The nurse who had broken the news to me hadn't given two shits about any menacing looks I'd thrown her way; she wasn't afraid of me. And though I feel like I'm crawling out of my skin waiting to hear news, I've felt better knowing the no-nonsense woman was caring for Blair behind those closed doors.

"Are you the man who came in with Blair Thompson?"

Blair Thompson. Before a couple of hours ago, I'd never heard that name before, so why does hearing it now make me feel like my very soul is tethered to those three syllables?

I nod, moving closer, suddenly unable to breathe. Even Walter lifts his head, his gaze focused on the doctor in front of me.

"We've checked her over. She took a nasty blow to the

head and has a mild concussion. The laceration on her temple took a few stitches, but it should heal up without leaving a scar. We're going to keep her here for observation, but Miss Thompson is going to be just fine."

Just fine. Those two words wash over me like a healing wave of relief, and finally, my lungs are able to function again.

It's funny. I've always thought of myself as a pretty level-headed guy. I think everything through, and never lead by emotions. But right now, my emotions are getting the best of me. All I want to do is push past the scrawny four-eyed doctor and rush into Blair's room, gather her in my arms, and tell her I'm so fucking sorry I let that son of a bitch get away. To promise her I'll find him and make him pay for what he did to her.

But I can't.

The fact is, even though I found her the way I did, and have spent hours on pins and needles waiting to hear that she's okay, Blair doesn't have the first fucking clue who I am. She doesn't know me. And with all the shit going on in my life, she doesn't want to know me. But I will find that fucker, and I will make him pay.

"Thank you," Judge says, breaking the awkward silence while I work out my thoughts. "Glad to hear the girl's gonna be fine."

The doctor's phone pings. Glancing at the screen, he nods and excuses himself, already off to deal with another patient. From our place in the lobby, we watch a group of uniformed officers, and a couple of detectives we all know far too well, walk toward Blair's room.

"What now?" Karma asks from behind me. "You gonna go back and claim the girl? Maybe see what it's like to bang a redhead in a hospital bed?"

Judge chuckles, but I don't find his shit joke funny at all. "No, asshole. We're gonna leave that girl to live her life in peace, but we're going to hunt this guy down. When we find him, he's going to pray to God he never darkened her doorstep. And we do it all before those fucking cops see us."

As I speak, Karma's teasing smile fades, and the seriousness of the situation fills the room once again. "Damn right," he mutters.

I grab Walter's leash, and with one last glance back at the corridor to Blair's room, we clear out, our mission the only thing I can concern myself with right now.

Chapter 5

BLAIR

APPARENTLY, signing myself out of the hospital against medical advice was never really an option. Not with the police barring me, not only from leaving the hospital, but from going home. My house is now an active crime scene, and until it's released from said status, my ass isn't going anywhere. Or so the balding, overweight detective currently taking up residence in the chair across from my bed tells me. We'll see about that. He has to go home sometime, and maybe the next officer on duty will be more sympathetic to my plight. A girl can hope, anyway.

You'd think having been attacked less than a day before would spare me from a constant barrage of questions. Between the medical staff, the police, and the reporters—who I've been told are camping in the parking lot in an attempt to get access to me—I'm at my wit's end. I need to rest, but that's not even in the realm of possibilities—or so it seems right now, with Detective Douchebag's line of questioning.

"Miss Thompson," the detective prompts. "Let's go over what you told me again."

"Blair. My name is Blair. Please use it," I interject coarsely. "What more is there to tell? It's not like you asking me the same questions over and over again is going to magically jog my memory."

Believe me, the possibility of me remembering much of anything is slim, outside years of therapy to unpack the trauma. I've studied cases like mine in my undergraduate classes. Some victims never remember, some do. The human brain is a minefield of complexities, and we've only begun scratching the surface when it comes to cognitive memory loss and the correlation of trauma-induced amnesia. But the detective seems hell-bent on proving both me and science wrong.

"Blair," he grumbles, correcting himself. "Can you describe your attacker?"

This again. This has to be the sixth or seventh time he's asked me that question since he walked in only an hour after I'd fully woken up. I didn't even get a chance to eat the now cold broth the nurse had been so kind to order for me. My hunger and well-being clearly comes second to this man.

"Detective, I've told you already. There was a guy

standing there, wearing a ski mask and holding a knife. He attacked, everything went black, I woke up here, and that's it."

He frowns, his disapproval spreading across his white, bearded face.

"I wish I could tell you more, but the entire thing is a blur in my head."

He grunts.

"You can grunt all you want, but it's not going to clear up the static in my head. I doubt even an aluminum foil wrapped bunny ear antenna could fix it. There's nothing there," I conclude.

He scowls then, rubbing his face in frustration. "Did you do anything to incite the man to attack?"

"Excuse me?"

"Many young college women these days bring unwanted attention upon themselves with the way they dress and act. It's not unheard of to attract the wrong kind of male attention."

"Are you kidding me right now?" I snap. "I was attacked in my own home, and you're victim blaming me like I'm some slut begging for it on the street?" Is he really insinuating I brought this on myself? That I flaunted myself at this man?

"Miss Thompson, you told me yourself you've posted fliers all around campus, looking to fill a vacancy in your home, and that you've invited numerous people to view it. You advertised your vulnerability for the entire world to see."

His words are like a punch in the gut. "You're a real piece of work. I'm an educated woman, Detective. Advertising for a roommate is *not* an open invitation for someone to invade my home and attack me."

He glares over at me. "From what I can tell, regarding the company you keep—if the man who called 911 is any indication—drawing that type of conclusion isn't far from the mark."

Here we go again. Why is everyone so interested in this guy? First, the nurse, and now the detective. It's a little difficult to talk about someone I've never met, or even seen.

"My answer hasn't changed from the last time you asked. I don't know him." I shrug. "He falls into that black area I just mentioned. I didn't even know anyone else was there." I point to my head, hoping it reminds him I'd taken a blow to it. This guy's a textbook ego-tripper. It almost makes me want to switch roles and pick his brain. *Almost.* I'm not sure I would want to poke around in there with his line of work. "I really want to help you, but there's only so much information I can offer."

"I see." Cool disbelief drips from his words. "It's just interesting to me that a complete stranger rushes into your house and saves your life, especially someone like this guy. He's not the kind of man that, as you said yourself, an 'educated woman' should associate themselves with."

It's odd, but I suddenly feel protective of my savior. "I'm not sure how to take that. How is a good Samaritan *interesting*? I owe everything to that man. Frankly, I think you should be thanking him instead of implying how 'interesting' it was he was there."

Unbelievable. This wasn't some kind of domestic dispute gone wrong. I was attacked in my own home, my life nearly taken. None of it was convenient for me—not one bit. And what is it about this man who's tripped the trigger for this detective? To be honest, the more he talks about him, the more I want to know. To get such ire after such a brave act is so odd. I just wish I'd gotten a chance to thank him.

"If you knew who he was, I doubt you'd be saying that, Miss Thompson. Men like him don't just save a woman's life without a purpose or a reason. I think you know more than you're telling me."

I go to argue, but he slaps his notebook closed. Apparently, the Q&A session is over.

"Instead of grilling me about a stranger—of which I have zero idea who he is or how he was there—why aren't you out on the streets, tracking down the person who did this?"

"It would be much easier to do if you'd cooperate, Miss Thompson," he replies through pursed lips. "It's very difficult to track someone down with only the description of a knife and dark eyes."

I straighten myself up in the bed, exerting far more labor than I had anticipated. *If it's a fight he wants, I'm now more than pissed off enough to give it to him.*

"Do your job, Detective. I can't give you any more information than what I've already told you."

"We're doing the best we can, Miss Thompson. It can take weeks for the blood evidence to process. And unless the suspect has any priors, it's like shooting fish in a barrel."

So that's it. All I can do is wait and hope this guy doesn't come knocking on my door again. This is unacceptable. It's not that I don't understand what the police department is trying to do, but there has to be some avenue they haven't thought of yet. There *has* to be.

"Someone had to have cameras up on their house. It's the damn suburbs, for goodness' sake. Do your job, and find him before someone else gets hurt." My chest heaves with anger, to the point that the pain from my head radiates through my entire body. The blood pressure monitor screams out an alarm, but he just stands there, staring at me like a father scolding his wayward daughter.

"What's going on here?" my nurse demands as she enters the room. She looks to me, then back to the detective, assessing the tension in the room. "Sir, upsetting my patient is a detriment to her recovery. I think you need to step out of the room and allow Miss Thompson to rest."

Thank you.

He stomps out of the room without a word, slamming the door behind him. It echoes off the walls for a few seconds after he leaves.

"That's better," she says with a smile. "I could hear him yelling at you from the nurse's station."

"He was a real peach, let me tell ya," I mutter, shifting painfully on the paper-thin mattress underneath me. "He could use some refresher training when it comes to interviewing a victim."

I shift again, trying to get comfortable, but it isn't going to happen. This hospital bed and I are not compatible. I'd heard about how awful they were, but experiencing the feeling of every spring poking into my ass for myself is a different story. These beds are cotton covered cement slabs with zero give or comfort to them.

"Your friend out in the waiting room didn't seem to like him either," she implies, moving over to the computer.

"My friend?"

She grins. "Mr. Tall, Dark, and Brooding out in the waiting room."

I frown. "I don't know who you're talking about."

"Well, whoever he is, it's a shame he left. The nurses out at the reception area didn't mind the view."

"Left?" Not that I care about the comings and goings of a complete stranger, but between the asshole detective and the nurses talking about him, I have to admit, they've piqued my curiosity.

"Sure did," she utters as she types away. "As soon as the detective arrived, he and all of his friends booked it out of here."

His friends? Who is this guy? And why does he have an entourage with him? It's troubling, for sure, but my heart still drops. He's gone without so much as a visit to see me. Why stay out there all this time and not come in? None of it makes sense. He could've at least stuck around long enough for me to thank him.

"I do have good news, though," the nurse says, shaking me from my unexpected heartache. "Dr. Malic is liking your numbers, and barring any unexpected complications, you should be getting out of here in the morning."

Going home. My stomach drops a second time. I should be excited—ecstatic, really—save for the fact that the person responsible is still out there. The news had already reported the victim of the attack had survived. So what's stopping him from coming back to finish the job? Maybe staying here a bit longer isn't so bad after all… well, if it weren't for Jinx. *Damn cat.*

The nurse shuffles around the room a few minutes more before she leaves again, advising the police guards at my door to allow me to rest for a few hours. She must be kidding if she thinks I'm going to sleep with the turmoil going on inside my head. There's too much to process. Do I stay there, or pack up Jinx and head to a hotel? A hotel would be safer, but costly. I'm not exactly rolling in cash without having someone to help pay the bills. And it's doubtful they'll be lining up to rent a spare room in the now almost murder house.

The rest of the afternoon trickles by slowly. It's not until after dinner that a new detective takes over, standing guard outside my door as if I'm a common criminal waiting to go back to jail instead of being the victim. At least this officer agreed to ask one of the patrolmen protecting my house to check on my cat. I failed to mention Jinx's temperament, but they'll figure it out soon enough if they try to pick her up.

I probably shouldn't have left that part out.

GREENPEACE

FOUR HOSPITALS, two days, and nothing. Not one single person has gone to the emergency room for a dog bite. And nothing for concussions, except for a couple of rowdy teenage football players. Which means we have nothing to go on. We still have no clue who this mother-fucker is, and Blair has officially been out of the hospital for twenty-four hours.

The worst part of all this is, it's been surprisingly difficult to stay away from her. We've never even had a conversation, but for some reason, I can't get the gorgeous redhead out of my mind. I feel protective of her —possessive, even—and the idea of her being unpro-tected while that son of a bitch is still out there has me on edge in a way I'm just not familiar with.

"Just one man," I say, my fists curled in frustration.

"Have him stay close enough to jump in, but far enough away she'll never know he's there."

Judge eyes me while he thinks over my request. "What is it about *this* girl? Why her?"

I've asked myself that same question over and over again, and have yet to come up with an answer that makes any sort of sense. "I don't know, man. I just feel she should be protected, ya know? Isn't that what we do?"

Judge crosses his arms over his chest, making his muscled biceps bulge. "Not fair, man. You know any one of the Black Hoods would lay his life down for someone who can't fight back, but we already have a mission. Those slimy fucks running the dog fights around here are back. They're bad news."

I glance down at Walter, who sits beside me, watching as if he's part of the conversation. The scar on his face and his missing eye came from a fight these same men had forced him in to. Catching them has been all I've thought about for months, until now.

"So, we only do one good deed at a time, then?"

Judge's face turns hard as stone. "What we're in to right now, GP? It's big time. You know it, and I know it. We can't turn back now, or we'll never put an end to these dog fights. And as for your girl, she's *not* your fucking girl. She has the cops involved. She has friends. Likely family. She's not alone. Shit will get handled without our help. We can't go getting involved in every little thing that happens in this town."

As much as I hate it, I can't argue with the man. Not only is he the president of the club, he's also one hundred percent right. Blair isn't mine. She's not my responsibility or my woman. Hell, she's not even my friend. I don't know her at all.

So why can't I let it go?

"We good?" Judge asks, tipping his beer bottle in my direction.

Reaching out, I tap his bottle with my own. "Yeah, man. We're cool."

"Good." Judge puts the bottle to his lips and drains the rest of its contents in one long pull. "Now, get outta here. I see a blonde over there who looks like she could use a little attention."

I glance behind me, scan the room for the blonde he's referring to, and spot her in the corner, her hair teased high, her dress practically painted on. "Wear a cock sock, bro," I warn, pushing up from the table. "That one's got a lot of experience with male attention."

Judge grins and plops his empty bottle down on the table, his eyes never leaving the woman across the room. "Always do, GP. Always do."

And that's the end of the conversation. I watch with amusement as Judge approaches the blonde, chuckling a little when her arms not-so-subtly push her tits together, making her cleavage more pronounced.

Oh, yeah. Judge is definitely going to need a cock sock.

I sit in silence for a few more minutes, my gaze wandering over the busy bar. All around me, people are laughing, drinking, and having a good time. More than a few of them call my name, inviting me to join them, but I nod and wave them off, not sure I can take on an actual conversation right now.

All I can think about is Blair. Is she home? Is she safe? Did she remember to lock her door? Are the police doing regular patrols?

Finally, I can't take it anymore. Digging into my pocket, I throw a twenty-dollar bill down on the table before heading through the crowd and out the door.

I get why Judge doesn't want to involve the club in whatever it is Blair's gotten mixed up in, but I can't stay uninvolved. I held this woman in my arms as she lay unconscious on her floor. I paced around the hospital while we waited for word from the doctors she was going to be all right.

Blair Thompson may not be my girl, but every freckle on her face is etched into my memory. I'll be damned if I'm gonna let anything happen to her. Club or no club, I'll personally make sure that asshole never gets within a hundred yards of her again.

BLAIR

"JINX!" I holler at the streak of black fur skidding away after nearly tripping me for the sixth time today. "I can't feed you if you trip and kill me!"

Jinx halts near the kitchen door, and peers back at me, licking her paw in absolute disinterest.

"Some friend you are," I mutter under my breath. I'm more like the butler to her furry highness as far as she's concerned.

Jinx trots off down the hall, disappearing with a *meow*. I roll my eyes at her insolence before turning back to wash the dirty dishes in the sink.

The minute I'd walked back into the house under the watchful eye of the douchebag detective and his band of not so merry junior detectives two days ago, she was my shadow. I can't use the restroom, eat, or even sleep—what little sleep I'm getting, anyway—without her pawing at me. At first, it was annoying, but now, it's oddly comforting to know someone cares enough to check up on me. Well, cares enough to make sure I'm still breathing and able to feed her, that is.

I'd tried to find an affordable hotel to relocate to for a few days so the police would have more time to track down my attacker, but my funds were too tight. Amazon had even failed me with affordable security systems. I can't afford a gun—though, if you asked just about any Texan, we should all be given one at birth, as common as they are around here. My grandmother was staunchly against them, and if anyone dared to cross her threshold with one holstered to their hip, she shooed them out with her broom until they put it elsewhere.

Staying put is my only option. To stay in the house where every thud, car going by, or noise outside makes my heart pound out of my chest and my skin crawl. The stain of my own blood on the hardwood floor may be gone from the naked eye, but it's still fresh in my mind. Bleach can't wipe away the emotional and mental stain, no matter how hard I try to put it out of my head.

He's still in there, torturing me from the inside. I can only hope that once my advising program professor is back in the office, she'll be willing to see me one-on-one to help me work through this.

Today has been much easier, though, aside from Jinx's aggressive attempts at affection. I spent most of the daylight hours asleep on the couch, with only a few instances of waking up in a panic when the loud roar of a motorcycle kept passing by the house in the early morning hours. I don't know who owns that thing, but they really need to find a different route to ride, and soon. Every rev of that engine put me on pins and needles, causing me to scramble off the couch. It took over an hour to calm myself down before I could finally fall asleep again.

Had my stomach not woken me up a few hours later, I might've slept through the entire evening and night.

Jinx rubs up against me while I cook dinner, begging for her own meal. I give in, as it's the only way I'm going to eat my own meal in peace.

I'm drying my hands at the sink when a sharp knock comes from the front door.

"Shit!" The unexpected intrusion sends my heart galloping at a pace that makes me sway on my feet. The towel falls into the soapy sink, sending bubbles flying up onto my shirt and face.

Breathe, Blair. It's broad daylight. He's not going to come back now. Not with the constant parade of patrol cars cruising by several times an hour.

I pad quietly to the edge of kitchen and peer down the hallway. The knocking comes again, but this time, with more force and intent. Moving one foot at a time, I inch closer to the door, breathing heavily with each step.

Looking through the peephole, I spy a man in a suit standing on the porch with a microphone in his hand, and a camera crew behind him.

"Miss Thompson," a male voice calls out. *Shit. He must've heard me. Shit. Shit. Shit.*

"What do you want?" My voice cracks as I move farther away from the front window, hiding behind the door with my back pressed against it.

"I'm Rich Van Nees with Channel Four News. I'd like to talk to you about your attack."

"No interviews," I call back, checking the lock. I doubt they would try to barge into my house, but I'm not about to take that chance. This guy's known for pushing his way into getting the impossible story. I remember watching the news with grandmother where he bum-rushed a physician accused of prescription drug abuse in the middle of an exam. This guy's the equivalent of an ambulance chasing scumbag lawyer.

"Miss Thompson, please. We want to tell your story."

"The police are handling my case. Talk to them. I can't give you anything more than their investigation can tell you.

"We want to talk to *you*." This time, I take notice of the annoyance in his voice.

He then mumbles for someone to ready their camera if I open the door. *Fat chance of that happening.* No good would come from me parading myself on the nightly local news. I don't need to paint a bigger target on my back, seeing as I'm continuing to remain at the scene of the crime. The beacon's bright enough on its own. The sooner reporters forget about my story, the better it'll be for me.

"The same can't be said for me, and I said no. Now, leave."

"Miss Thompson, please reconsider. We can help each other."

"The only thing you can help me with is escorting yourself off my property before I call the police and report you for unlawful trespassing and harassment. You can also relay that message to the others who are out there with you. I'll not be giving you or anyone else an interview. You're wasting your time."

He swears under his breath before stomping off the porch, with a gaggle of footsteps trailing behind him. Walking into the living room as quickly as I can without causing myself pain, I push aside the curtains just enough to get a better view of my front yard.

Four different news vans line the street. Two of them have cameramen and reporters outside of them. Van Nees continues down the sidewalk and throws his hands up when another reporter calls out to him. Yet, none of them leave. I watch for over an hour as each one of them positions themselves on the sidewalk outside of my house, recording their news report, basically telling my attacker right where to find me. *This is not what I need right now.*

Sliding my cell phone from my pocket, I dial the number the douchebag detective had given me.

"Detective Morrison," he snaps.

"Detective, this is Blair Thompson."

"Ah, Miss Thompson," he drawls. "Finally ready to tell me about your friend at the hospital?"

Seriously? "What is it with you and this guy? I have zero ties to him, okay? None. Zip. Zilch. Zero."

"I know you're not being honest with me. Guys like him don't just go saving random women. There's a reason, and I'd like to know what it is."

"How many damn times do I have to say it?" I holler into the phone, my reason for calling him in the first place disappearing from my mind. "I don't know him. I don't know who he is or why you have such a hard-on for him, but every minute you focus on him is another minute my attacker is still out there, possibly hurting some other innocent woman. Why haven't you caught him?"

Every inch of my body tingles with rage. I'm the victim, but this son of a bitch is intent to believe otherwise. I don't know how much more of his victim-blaming I can subject myself to before I snap. I am *not* at fault. I didn't cause this man to attack me. I just wish the detective would pull his head out of his ass and see that for himself. As long as my attacker roams free, my life is at risk, and my sense of safety deteriorates even more.

"We're trying our best. If you don't have any information to add to your case, what can I do for you? Did someone else follow you home?" Blatant teasing reverberates in his tone.

I clench my teeth, trying to keep my cool. Snapping at him won't to get me any more help than he's already doling out. I don't know if they teach misogyny at the academy, but if they did, this guy aced it.

"I'd like to have an officer sent to my house."

"Can I ask why?" he huffs in disbelief. "I'm not going to waste department resources on someone who isn't even willing to help herself by telling the truth."

"Jesus," I mutter. Heavy knocking starts at my door again. Raising my arm, I hold my cell phone toward the sound so he can hear it. "That knocking you hear is a group of reporters currently camping out in front of my house. I'd like them to leave and stop knocking on my door."

"Knocking on a door isn't a crime, Miss Thompson. They're just trying to do their jobs, much like I'm trying to do mine. I see you're being just as uncooperative with them."

"Listen, asshole," I snarl. "I've been attacked, hospitalized, harassed by you, and now I'm being harassed by reporters. If you don't send someone over here to make them leave, I'll go on camera and call you and your entire department out for not doing your job."

He attempts to argue with me, but I hang up before he can get the first word out. *Should I have called the lead detective on my case an asshole?* Probably not, but I'm at my wit's end. My life is in shambles, and I'm emotionally and physically drained. Something has to give, and if I have to threaten an officer of the law to get it done, so be it.

Apparently, though, it worked, because less than thirty minutes later, all four vans are peeling out of their parking spaces.

Peace and haunting quiet at last. But it's a stinging reminder that I'm truly alone in this world, except for Jinx. I'd be lying if I said I hadn't thought of being alone. That I'd be fine with no one to miss me if I'd died that day. My parents left me, and so did my roommates. Grandmother was the only one I had left in this world until cancer stole her away from me.

Truth be told, I'm the poster child for being abandoned when you need support the most. It had taken years to work through my childhood abandonment trauma with multiple therapists, and now, that deeply seated fear is returning all over again.

Am I even deserving of love?

GREENPEACE

I LEAN AGAINST MY MOTORCYCLE, attempting to appear casual, as Jack Carson pulls into his driveway. I can tell just by the set of his jaw he knows exactly why I'm here. This is going to get interesting.

He unfolds his scrawny frame from the driver's seat and slams the door closed. "May I help you?"

Standing, I take a couple of steps forward, but stop when his fists clench and move toward his waist. He and I both know he's packing, and I'm not about to get shot. "Just a friendly visit, Carson. Why so jumpy?"

"Fuck you," he spits back, his eyes flashing with rage. "We aren't friends. What the hell do you want?"

All right, time to cut the shit. "We know the Armstrong boys are still running fights. I wanna know when and where. No bullshit."

Carson's face pales, but I have to give him credit. His

expression doesn't falter in the least. "I don't know what the fuck you're talking about, man. I don't have anything to do with the Armstrongs anymore." His eyes dart toward the house, and I follow his gaze to see a little girl peering out the window, her crooked grin beaming brightly down at us. He waves up at her with a smile, barely moving his lips as he says, "Please don't make a scene in front of my girl."

Leverage. Dirty leverage, but it's all I've got. "Then answer my fucking question, Carson. Where are the fights, and when?"

His arms fly up in exasperation. "I fucking told you, man, I don't know shit, okay? The last time the Black Hoods broke that shit up, the Armstrongs went ballistic. My wife told me she'd take the kids and leave town if I didn't get away from them. I haven't had a thing to do with them since."

I look behind me at the house where the little girl waves back at me, her smile so wide, I can't help but wave back. "Cute kid," I tell him. "Would be a shame for her to lose her daddy because he doesn't know when to tell the truth. Judge isn't backing down, Carson. None of us are. The Black Hoods are going to end this shit, with or without your help. And if you're involved, you'll go down with them."

Carson sighs, his shoulders slumping with defeat.

I hold my ground as he steps around his truck and comes closer.

"Look, I'm serious. I don't have anything to do with them. Not anymore. The Armstrongs are fucking crazy, and my family comes first. But I'll tell you one thing." His head swivels from side to side, his eyes scanning the area around us. "I heard it from a guy who still works for them that they've been building a ring outside of Paloma, back in the bush somewhere."

I stare at him, trying like hell to gauge if he's telling me everything he knows.

"Keep my name out of it. I can't get involved in this shit again, man. Not if I want to keep my family. I suggest you talk to Kenny Dwyer. He'll know way more than me."

And there it is. Carson offering up a name, like that tells me he's trying to get his shit together for real. "Appreciated," I tell him, then take a step back. "Your name's nowhere near it. I'll let the club know you're trying to turn your life around, but if I even hear a whisper about you anywhere near this, the Black Hoods will rain hell down on you, family or no family. You hear me?"

Carson swallows, nodding up and down like an oversized bobble head. "I hear you."

Having said all I need to say, I throw my leg back over the seat and fire up my bike. It's not much, but the info he just gave me is more than we've learned in over a week of researching. Judge will be happy. It puts us one step closer to nailing the motherfuckers who tortured Walter, and God knows how many other defenseless dogs. The Armstrong brothers' days are numbered.

I'm also hoping this new info will keep Judge off my back a little bit. The bastard seems intent on keeping me busy, knowing damn well I'm not listening to his orders to steer clear of Blair. He hasn't mentioned it yet, but he's working hard to keep me from checking up on her by tasking me to run errands over the last few days. Tasks that should be put on the prospects, not a member. But I had no choice, as he's my president. He just doesn't need to know about my extracurricular activities.

I was right to keep watching her, though. Judge was way off when he said she had someone. I've been watching her house like some kind of creeper for days, and aside from the occasional police drive-by, and the gaggle of reporters who won't back the fuck off, she's been completely alone.

Dangerously alone. And fuck me, there's no way I'm going to leave her that way. No matter how much Judge doesn't want the club involved, I *am* involved, with or without them to back me up. Blair's safety is on my shoulders now.

Usually, driving my motorcycle has a way of soothing my swirling thoughts, but not today. I make it to my house in what feels like no time at all, and I still haven't stopped thinking about how fucked-up all of this is.

Once I've parked and closed the garage door, I pull out my cell phone and give Judge a call.

"What did you find out?" his gruff voice barks over the heavy beats of music playing in the background.

"Well, hello to you too, buddy."

"Cut the shit, GP. What'd you find?"

I sigh, scrubbing a hand along my face. "Not as much as we'd hoped. Carson's out of the game, for real this time. But he did give me a name to follow up on, and he did say that wherever they're rebuilding is outside Paloma somewhere."

"Paloma, eh?" I can practically hear the wheels turning in his head. "You sure he's out? He was in fucking deep that last time."

I picture that little girl in the window, and the fear on Carson's face. "I'm sure. His old lady threatened to take their kids. He won't risk that."

"Think he's lying?"

"He nearly pissed himself when his kid came out. Pretty sure he was telling the truth."

Judge chuckles into the receiver. "Fair enough. See what you can find out about the contact he gave you. The longer these fuckers have time to organize, the more work we'll have to handle."

"Ain't that the truth."

"You coming back to the clubhouse tonight?"

A muffled female voice says something quietly in the background, officially removing Judge from this conversation. Thank fuck.

"Nah," I say, already walking to my front door. "Walter's been cooped up in the house all day. Think I'm going to stay home and take the poor bastard for a walk."

"You're turning down Grade A pussy for your dog? Wouldn't have anything to do with the sexy redhead-in-distress being home now, would it?"

Shit. Has he been checking up on me?

"Nah, Judge." I have to force the words out. "She isn't the club's problem." Every syllable burns as I voice it. Lying to my president isn't something I take lightly. Judge has always been there for me, so it's a punch to the gut doing this behind his back. But leaving Blair isn't an option for me.

"Let's keep it that way. Not the time to be bringing new blood around the club."

"Roger that, Prez." I have no intention of bringing Blair into the club life. Girls like her don't need the taint we smear all over the place. Once she's safe, I'll bail. Simple as that.

"Good," he declares, the word more of an order than an agreement. The same soft voice makes a noise in the background. "One second, sweetheart," Judge tells her.

"GP, get on tracking down Carson's buddy. No time to waste."

I nod, even though he can't see me. I'm just glad to have the conversation turned away from Blair. "You got it. Have fun tonight."

"Always do, man," he says with another chuckle. "Later."

Knowing him as well as I do, he'll be drunk and balls deep in pussy very shortly, which is a good thing for me, because once I let Walter out, I have my own girl to go see.

Chapter 9

BLAIR

"HEY, BLAIR," another graduate assistant whispers. This chick may be in my program, but she's never paid a lick of attention to me before now. I try to ignore her, but she pokes one of her fingers into my side to get my attention. "Psst, Blair."

"I'm trying to listen to the lecture," I whisper through clenched teeth. Why can't she take the hint that I have zero interest in answering whatever question she's so adamant in asking me?

A student behind us leans down and shushes her, annoyance clear as day painted across her face as she points to the professor at the front of the room. My inquisitor slumps back into her seat with a thud. I peek over my shoulder and give a thankful nod to my savior, Lindsey—one of the few original students in my program who hadn't transferred out before the graduate program began.

"Thanks," I whisper, and she smiles back.

Coming back to my classes was by far one of the biggest decisions I've languished over the last few days since my release from the hospital. Professor McCallen had been very clear in her email response that my return to the summer program schedule was not something set in stone if I didn't feel up to returning. Ready, I'm not, but the only way of finding my sense of normalcy again is by not putting my life on hold.

I settle back into my seat, focusing on the lecture being presented on handling patients with histories of violence and abuse with respect—one that hits a little too close to home right now. Outside of the nurses, respect was the last word I would use to describe my treatment during my ordeal.

The rest of the seminar goes by peacefully, but whether it's my imagination or not, I feel like the other students are paying more attention to me than the professor. I feel like a freak on display in the middle of a crowded room as the girl who survived. Though calling myself that seems a bit too much like a second-generation Harry Potter villain.

The second the lecture is over, I gather my belongings and bolt toward the door before anyone else can corner me. But that's when I find Lindsey, leaning against the doorjamb, waving for me to join her. She'd saved me back there. It would be rude to ignore her and walk past now, as much as I would like to do just that.

"Hey." I force a smile. "Thanks for shutting up that girl back there."

"Not a problem," she replies. "You don't deserve that shit. Look, I have about an hour before my ride gets here. Want to grab a bite?" She glances over her shoulder toward the large vending machine area.

I hate to turn her down, but this is my first day back, and I'm exhausted. "As much as I'd like that, I really want to get home before it gets too dark."

"I understand. Here, take this." Reaching into her purse, she pulls out a pen and a piece of paper, scribbles something down and hands it to me. "This is my cell phone number. If you want to talk, or, whatever, feel free to text me."

I peer down at the slip of paper in my hand. *I don't get it?* "Thanks. But I have to ask… why are you being so nice to me? We barely know each other."

Lindsey's lips turn up in a sad smile. "Freshman year, I was in your shoes."

"You were attacked?" I gasp.

She nods and slides her long, dark hair away from her shoulder, revealing a long scar across her neck that trails up and onto her left cheek. "Football player. I said no, and he didn't like it. He attacked me in the parking lot of his frat house, and tried to put my face through the windshield of a car when I fought back."

"Oh, my God!" I gasp. What else can I say? How did I not see that in the paper? Football is life here in Texas, and if this guy played for our team, it should've been front page news.

"It sucked ass," she says. "But I had help. I'd like to help you if you need it."

Her phone chimes loudly, taking her gaze away from mine, and grimaces at the screen. "Shit. My car broke down this morning, and now my ride's bailing on me. The last bus to my apartment complex is like, now, so I gotta run." She starts to turn, but stops. "Seriously, Blair. Call me if you want to talk."

"I will. Thank you," I call out before she disappears out the door.

I don't make it far before I run headlong into Professor McCallen in the hallway, knocking the book in her hand to the ground.

"I'm so sorry, Professor. I wasn't watching where I was going," I apologize, but she throws up her hand, stopping me.

"It's fine, Blair. I was hoping to run into you today. Well, not literally. Do you have a few minutes?" She gestures to her office.

"Of course," I reply. Pivoting on her heels, I follow her through the open door of her office.

"Please, close the door behind you and take a seat."

Professor McCallen sits behind her desk, depositing her book onto the large pile next to her. I slide into the open chair across from her. I've been to her office at least a half dozen times this year alone to discuss the program, and for one-on-one counseling sessions. This visit feels different, though.

"Blair, I know that you've been through a traumatic experience. The department and I want to make sure that returning to your studies is the best course of action for you at this time. Balancing a full doctoral program schedule is hard enough, but you're also working as a teaching assistant. I just want to make sure you're not only physically, but also emotionally capable of jumping back into the saddle, as they say."

"I understand, Professor," I tell her. "But getting my life back is the only way I'm going to get through this."

Her assessing stare never leaves mine. She must be searching for cracks in the armor I spent the entire morning walling up to face today. I have to stay strong. My studies are all I have to cling to to take my mind off the fact that I'm facing all of this alone.

"Blair, I only want what's best for you. You're by far one of this year's most talented students in the first year doctoral program. But if you need to take a sabbatical, the program committee has already agreed to hold your spot for a year if you need it."

"And I appreciate that, but to me, this isn't negotiable. I'm not going to let this guy take my life away from me. I've worked too hard to get here."

She folds her hands together on her desk with an unreadable look crossing her face, making me second guess my decision. Am I doing the right thing?

"I thought that might be what you would say, but the offer still stands. If you find yourself overwhelmed at any point, Blair, my office is always open to you. Seeing you succeed in your work is something I take great interest in. If you, for any reason at all, need to vent, talk, unpack your feelings, I'm here for you. I hope you truly know that."

Sincerity rings true in her voice. I've always felt especially close with her since the day I landed in her office as her undergraduate advisee. Today, she feels like the only person in the world who has my back, and the overwhelming urge to make her proud reverberates through every fiber of my being. Failure is not an option for me—it never has been—but now, even more so.

"I do," I assure her. "I know that the days and weeks ahead aren't going to be easy, but I think I can handle it. Honestly, school isn't worrying me. I've wanted to be a psychologist for as long as I can remember. It's my dream, and I'm not about to mess it up now that I'm so close."

"Staying positive is key to recovering from trauma such as yours, but you also need to remember not every day is going to be a good one. You'll have ups and downs. It's natural for the mental and emotional healing process."

"I understand, Professor McCallen, I really do. This is just a speed bump."

"A violent one, Blair. There's a difference," she interjects. "Have the police made any headway in your case?"

I go on to tell her about my experience with the detective leading my case, and she gives me the name and number of a few personal contacts she has within the police department who I can contact if his unacceptable behavior toward me continues.

I really want to stay and talk to her more, but another student bursts through the door, begging to speak with her. I politely excuse myself and exit her office, starting down the hallway.

Halfway to the door, my roommate flier on the community board stops me in my tracks. After everything the detective had said to me earlier, I turn to examine it. *Was it my fault? Did I advertise my vulnerability?* I reach out to yank it off the corkboard when a conversation around the corner catches my attention.

"I can't believe Blair showed her face here today."

My heart drops. I inch closer to the corner, my ears straining, knowing full well the more I hear, the more it will hurt to listen.

"She looks like shit. Did you see her jump when someone's book fell off their desk? I thought she was going to cry in the middle of lecture," a second voice jokes.

"I mean, do you blame her?" a third voice chides, but this one at least seems to be more understanding. "She's been through hell. Cut her some slack."

"Oh, come on!" the first voice whines, her words dripping with condescension. "You can't believe her story. It's all over Twitter that she's lying."

"The cops say they have no motive or suspects," someone else chimes in. "It's like the dude was a ghost."

"Or someone she knew," the first voice adds.

Slowly, I peer around the corner, spying at least six of my classmates huddled together like a high school clique.

"Would it surprise you? She lives in that big house all by herself. No one would know if she's living a double life. It's not like she has any real friends."

They dig and dig until I can't take it anymore. I step around the corner and face my accusers head-on. Enough is enough. Every one of them look like deers in headlights when they realize I heard every vile word that just came out of their mouths.

"Shit," the girl who sat next to me this morning gasps when she spots me staring a hole through them.

"Just stop," I order, throwing up a hand.

"We didn't mean…" she stammers.

It's odd that when they thought I couldn't hear them, gossiping about my situation was fine. But as soon as they're faced with the person who, until just a few minutes ago was the butt of their jokes, they clam up.

I don't respond. It's not like they would listen, anyway. I leave them there to contemplate their decision to verbally beat down someone who can't go any lower emotionally. I make it down the stairs of the building before hot, wet tears begin running down my face. How can educated people who don't even know me shove such accusations my way? Especially those who should ethically help people in my situation, not shame them?

"Hey, Blair!" someone calls out from behind me, but I ignore them. I can't deal with anything else today. Turning to the sidewalk, I start for home.

The farther I get from campus, the streets become quieter, and with the eerie silence, my nerves begin to frazzle. Heavy footsteps approach me from behind at a brisk pace, and my mind pleads with me to run. I turn to face them, only to find a delivery driver jogging off to the house I just passed to drop off a package.

Get a grip on yourself, Blair. Not everyone's out to get you.

Just a psychopath who tried to kill you in your own home, and who knows if he's even still around?

A few minutes later, home finally comes into view. My instinct is to bolt toward the door, but I keep my head high and my shoulders back, determined to keep my composure. Once I get inside, then I can lose my shit. But not out here.

A shadow moves in the hedges just off my front porch. Screeching to a halt, I duck behind a tree trunk and peer around it, my eyes straining to see more clearly. *Please let it be my imagination.*

The shadow moves again. *Oh, God.* I fumble to get my phone out of my pocket, not sure whether I should call the detective or 911, but it doesn't matter. The battery is dead. *Fuck.*

I never take my eyes off the shadowy form. *What should I do? Do I run? Do I confront him?*

The shadow moves away from the hedges, disappearing around the side of the house and out of sight. A passing truck startles me, pulling my attention away from the shadow, and that's when I spy a motorcycle parked outside the house next to mine. An empty house. Could it be the same motorcycle that keeps making laps around my house at all hours of the night, or just a coincidence?

What the hell do I do? I can continue to be a victim and run away, or I can stand my ground. My heart thunders against my ribs the longer I watch from a safe distance, waiting for the shadow to reappear.

As I wait, my muscles tense, and anger begins to burn a hole deep in the pit of my stomach. *No.* If the world is going to blame me, I'm not going to be the victim anymore. Nobody is going to protect me, so it's time I protect myself.

Who does this asshole think he is, anyway? He breaks into my house, assaults me, puts me in the hospital, and haunts every waking moment of my life with the fear of him returning to finish what he'd started, and now he's here.

Not this time, asshole.

I tiptoe out from behind my hiding spot, my lungs burning from holding my breath. I spy a large branch from a pile of brush my neighbor collected and grab it. At least I'll have a weapon this time and know it's coming.

As if in slow motion, I lay my book bag down on the edge of the porch and sneak around to where the man went, careful not to make a sound. At the corner, I press my back against the wall, clutching the heavy branch to my chest. *You can do this, Blair.*

Leaning forward, I peek my head around, and there he is, just a few feet away, standing in my back yard. He's looking down at his phone, as if he doesn't have a goddamn care in the world.

Bastard. Pulling the branch away from my body, I take three giant steps and swing back. The branch comes forward, aimed for his head. A cry escapes my throat the likes of which I've never heard before. Just before the branch connects, the man turns, and I see his face for the very first time.

Chapter 10

GREENPEACE

I DON'T EVEN THINK *she's home.*

I peer through the branches of shrubbery and wait a little longer. When I'd first gotten here, there'd been so many damn reporters, all of them looking to score the story of the week. That isn't going to happen.

Blair needs time to heal. To recover. Not to have a bunch of fucking paparazzi following her around like she's OJ goddamn Simpson.

All it took was a quick warning and a flash of the club's patch on my back for them to take me seriously and get lost. After threatening to remove the one guy's ballsack and feed it to his cameraman, I doubt any of them will be back.

If she's not home, why am I even here?

I've been scouting around quite a bit lately, doing what I can to keep Blair safe from a distance. But skulking outside her house when she's not even home is getting a bit too stalkerish, even for me.

One peek inside, just in case. After doing a few security sweeps of her yard, I discovered I can see directly into her living room from her back yard. The patio door is wide, and I've yet to see the curtains closed. Not something I approve of, but it's handy to ensure she's safe when she's home.

Sticking to the shadows, I make my way to the back yard, just to the left of the patio door. Darkness. No signs of Blair at all. Though her cat's another story. It's stretched out in a bright strip of sunlight that shines down onto the floor, its ears flat to its head while it stares at me through the leaves of the bush between us.

My phone buzzes in my pocket.

Karma: Judge is on a rampage. Come quick.

Fuck. I don't know what's been up Judge's ass lately, but he's been extra ornery the past couple of weeks. He's stressed about the Armstrong brothers popping up again and rejuvenating their dog fighting business—hell, all of us are—but he's been like an angry old bear, fresh out of hibernation, and it's starting to wear thin on all of us.

A bellowing cry, one that would make any Xena fan proud, assaults my ears from behind, and I turn just before something connects with the side of my head, mashing my ear into my skull.

"Fucking hell!" I press my hand to my ear and glare

at the attacker, the anger draining from me in an instant when I see who it is.

Blair stands before me, her red curls messy and wind-blown, her shoulders heaving as she tries to catch her breath. "Stay back, asshole."

Her tone is strong and confident, and if her hands weren't trembling while clutching the branch she smashed me with, I'd almost believe she was fearless. "I've already called the police," she says. "They're on their way."

Ignoring the pain in my throbbing ear, I lower my hand and pat the air between us. "Calm down, sweet-heart. I'm not here to hurt you."

Blair's nostrils flare, and she takes a step back, waving the branch between us. "I'm not your *sweetheart*," she spits back. "What do you want from me?"

I drop my hands, trying to appear as calm and unthreatening as possible. "I was just making sure you were safe, that's all."

Her freckled nose crinkles with disbelief. "Making sure I was safe? Bullshit. You were creeping around outside my house like a fucking stalker."

I can't take my eyes off her freckles. Off her face. Blair's a gorgeous woman, but when she's angry like this... Fuck me, she's adorable.

Blair draws back the branch, ready to swing again. "Hey, asshole, stop staring."

The chuckle escapes my lips before I can stop it, and her eyes flash with fury. "You think this is a joke? I will fucking bash your skull in!"

"I'm sure you would," I say, both trying and failing to contain my grin. "I'm sure you're very deadly with that... stick of yours. But I'm not here to hurt you. I was just checking in. I've been doing it every day since..."

The rage in her eyes falters a little before falling away completely, replaced by understanding. "You," she whispers. "You're him. The one who saved me that night."

My smile fades at the memory. Blair, bloody and crumpled on the floor. I can't answer, so I simply nod.

Lowering the branch, she holds it low at her side. "Why?" she asks. "How? How did you save me? Why didn't you stay?"

I sigh, pointing to the steps of her deck. "May I?"

I can tell she's still unsure about me, but she nods, nonetheless. Taking a seat, I again suppress a laugh at her standing there, the stick in her hand still between us. "It was my dog," I tell her. "He must've heard you scream, and he wasn't giving me any choice but to check it out."

Her eyes widen. "So you stopped him?"

I nod. "And the dog got a good bite or two in, so whoever he is, he's hurting."

"Did you see who it was?"

I sigh and drop my head, unable to look at her. "No. I

almost had him, but you were hurt so fucking bad. You needed help, so I focused on you. I hate I let that fucker get away, though."

The stick lands on the ground with a gentle thud, and she takes a seat beside me on the step, the heat of her body radiating against my arm. "I could have died."

I lift my head and meet her electrifying green eyes. "I know."

"Thank you."

The words come out as a whisper, but I feel them deep in my soul.

"No thanks needed, Red. I'm just glad we got here when we did."

Her eyes brighten, and a small smile graces her lips. We stay that way far longer than necessary, just staring at each other.

"Why didn't you stay?" she asks. "At the hospital. They told me you were out there, but that once they told you I was okay, you left."

I focus my gaze down and scratch at an imaginary stain on my worn jeans. "We didn't know each other. I didn't want to make it weird."

Her tiny hand comes into view, forcing my attention back to her. "Blair," she offers with a smile.

Taking her hand in mine, I do my best not to notice how fragile and perfect it feels there while giving it a slow shake.

"GP," I reply.

She tilts her head to the side, her nose scrunching with confusion. "GP?"

"Short for GreenPeace," I explain. "It's what my friends call me."

Her smile grows wider, her teeth shining through the crease between her full, pink lips. "Well, GP, now we know each other."

I chuckle, her soft hand still in mine. "Yes, we do."

My phone buzzes again. *Fuck. Judge.*

"I gotta go." I release my grip on her hand and force myself to stand. Touching her was a mistake, but fuck did her skin feel good. "Give me your phone and I'll put my number in." *Fuck, that sounds weird.* "You know... in case you need something."

She pats her pocket, and then stops. "It's dead."

I frown. "So how the fuck did you call the cops?"

Her shoulders lift in a shrug, and her smile reappears. "I lied."

"Jesus," I mutter. She was going to go after her attacker with a fucking branch and no goddamn back up. She's either brave or extremely lucky it was me checking up on her and not the guy coming back to finish the job. Either way, I might just have to come by more often to make sure she hasn't tried this stunt on someone else. "Pen?"

Blair pops up from the step and motions for me to

follow her. We go around to the front of the house where her book bag lies against the front step. She bends over to unzip it, and I can't take my eyes off her ass. *Quit it, dumbass. Stop looking at what you can't have.*

"Here you go." She offers me a bright pink pen and a heart-shaped Post-it note.

I stare at the two items. I can honestly say that in all my life, I've never before had anything so fucking girly in my hands. "Jesus," I mutter again, ignoring her giggle as I scribble my information onto the paper. "Call me," I tell her, my tone as serious as a heart attack. "Day or night, rain or shine. I live just around the corner, and can be here way faster than the police can."

"Thank you," she says softly, gripping the paper in her hand.

I take a step toward the sidewalk and lift my hand in a wave. "See ya, Blair."

"See ya, GP."

Jesus. She's trouble with a capital T.

Chapter 11

BLAIR

IT'S BEEN three days since GP revealed himself as my savior, and I can't seem to get him out of my head. It still boggles my mind that a complete stranger would throw himself *and* his dog into danger to help me. It makes zero sense to me. Yet he did without a second thought.

Who does that? And to give me his number in case I needed to contact him? I should've thrown it away the second he left, but here I am, days later, still staring at it like an idiot. He could be my attacker, for crying out loud, and I'm considering texting him and inviting him into my house like a friend.

What is wrong with me?

The worst is that a part of me wants to. It would take two hands to count the number of times I clicked on his name and started to text him. I type one after another, but then quickly delete each one like some smitten teenage girl who wants to tell her crush how much she likes him.

Pathetic, I know. But unless you count that cute neighbor boy I had a crush on when I was just a kid, and the one guy I dated during freshman year who kicked me to the curb a millisecond after he started rushing a fraternity, I have zero adult experience in this arena. After I got dumped, I focused on my schoolwork, and decided to forget all about the dating scene. Then GP rescued me, and now all that hard work isn't even factoring into my thoughts anymore.

One thing bothers me, though. He burst into my life, and he's a complete stranger. I've met the man once—twice if I count the attack—and I can count the things I know about him on one hand.

His name, sort of. GP. A nickname, I'm guessing, but who knows in this day and age? People name their kids after vegetables and fruits now. It might very well be his real name for all I know.

That he's been the one checking up on me at all hours of the night with his loud motorcycle, and that he lives nearby. Though after going at him with a stick, I haven't seen him around since. Not that I've been looking. Okay, fine, I have been looking. Constantly looking, if I'm being honest here.

And I've seen his face. A handsome one, with sharp

angles and dark eyes I could feel staring directly into my soul. It's a face I wouldn't mind looking at on a regular basis.

That's it. The fact of the matter is, I really don't know this guy, but try telling that to my brain, which keeps playing our first meeting over and over again. Yet, here I am, with GP still on my mind, like some love-sick girl. *What the hell is wrong with me?*

"Stop thinking about him," I mutter to myself, peering up into the still steamy mirror from my nightly shower. I wish it were that simple—to say the magic words and all thoughts and dreams I've had of him over the past few days would disappear. I can't get that lucky.

My fingers trace the light bruises splattered across my face. The final reminder of what I've been through physically beginning to fade from dark purple to a shade of yellow. Shaking both the wounds and GP from my head, I wrap my fluffy bath towel around myself. Stepping out of the bathroom and into my bedroom, Jinx greets me at the door with a sharp hiss.

"Stop that," I scold her. Her furry black behind rubs against my leg, growling as she does. She's been on edge much more today than she was the day I came home from the hospital. Any sound or movement from outside sends her into a fit of angry hisses and growls within a few seconds.

"What's wrong?" I coo, giving her a scratch between

the ears. She howls even louder, staring straight at the door of my bedroom. A feeling of extreme uneasiness washes over me the longer she postures in one specific direction. "Did you hear something down there?"

I scan the room. *Wait…*

The clothes laid out on my bed before getting in the shower are strewn across the floor. It's been years since Jinx has done something like this. I want to believe this mess is her doing, but that all changes when I see the top drawer of my dresser ajar. There's no way she could've managed that. Someone's been in my room.

Jinx lowers her frame closer to the ground and inches to my door. She peeks outside, and a loud crash echoes from downstairs. *I'm not alone.*

"Fuck," I scream under my breath. Grabbing Jinx from the doorway, I run back into the bathroom, and quickly lock the door behind me. My fingers tremble as I reach for my phone on the counter, my entire body trembling while trying to jab at the numbers.

"Pick up, pick up, pick up," I plead into the receiver, until the detective's gruff voice answers.

"Ready to tell me about your boyfriend, Miss Thompson?" Detective Morrison chides.

"No! This is really an emergency. Someone's in my house!"

"Slow down, Blair," he says, his tone a little more alert than before. "Tell me what happened."

"Someone ransacked my room while I was in the shower."

"Do you know if they're still in the house?"

"I think they're downstairs. I keep hearing noises."

"Where are you right now?" he asks, but then he's talking to someone else, barking out orders.

"Locked in my bathroom. Please hurry," I beg, with tears streaming down my face. "I'm trapped if they're still in the house."

"Sit tight," he insists. "I'm on the other side of town working another case, but I'll get dispatch to send officers to your house as quickly as I can. Stay where you are, and stay quiet."

"How long?" I ask tearfully.

"I don't know," he answers truthfully. "But I promise you, someone will be there as fast as they can."

He hangs up. Without a timetable of when help will arrive, I'm a sitting duck if I wait for his officers to show up. *It'll be too late.*

My heart races, and I try to force my breathing to even out. I'm on the brink of a panic attack.

"Call me. Day or night, rain or shine. I live just around the corner, and can be here way faster than the police can."

GP's promise rings through my memory, and I pull up his contact info. *Please be close enough to help me now.* He saved me once before. I just have to hope he'll do it a second time.

"Blair?" GP answers, but I can barely hear him with the noise in the background.

"Someone's in my house," I whisper into the phone with my hand cupping the receiver.

"What did you say? Hang on a second, sweetheart. Let me get outside. I can barely hear you." The noise disappears, and he speaks again. "I can hear you now. You okay?"

"Someone's in my house," I repeat. "I called the cops, but they aren't here yet. Please, I'm scared," I word vomit, but a second loud crash from downstairs scares me enough to scream. "They're still in the house!"

"I'm on my way, sweetheart. I need you to listen to me, okay? Stay quiet. I'll be there as quick as I can, you hear me?" The sound of a motorcycle firing up booms into the speaker.

"Yes," I cry. "Hurry."

"I'm coming for you right now, baby," he croons. He hangs up just as a third noise comes from downstairs. This time, it comes from directly below my bathroom.

I freeze, squeezing Jinx tightly against me. *Please let GP make it in time*. The seconds pass like hours, spanning eons in real time without the roar of a motorcycle or the sound of sirens.

"Stay calm, Blair. Just stay calm. GP and the cops are on the way. Just keep breathing," I whisper to myself and

Jinx, until the sound of the stairs creak under ascending heavy footsteps.

The odds were in my favor the last time, but would that ring true the second?

Chapter 12

GREENPEACE

MOVE, *asshole.* I slide my motorcycle between two lanes of traffic. I'm being totally reckless, but I don't really give a shit right now.

He's in her house.

Of all the nights for me to be at the fucking club-house. I usually don't stick around after a meeting, but Judge was still on the warpath, and I didn't want to chance pissing him off even more. What I should've done was gone straight home. Well, straight to Blair's, to make sure all was well.

Zooming onto the off ramp, a horn screams in my ear. I narrowly avoid taking out the front end of a sedan, but the near miss barely registers. *If Blair's attacker is in the house, I'm going to kill that motherfucker this time.*

The subdivision is quiet at this hour of night, though lights still blaze in most of the houses that line the streets. All except Blair's. Only one light's on in an upstairs window.

I screech to a halt in front of her house before clambering off my motorcycle. I take the porch stairs two at a time, and my heart stutters in my chest when I find the front door not only unlocked, but open a full two feet. Darkness and silence lay beyond it.

My hand tightens around my Glock 17, and I pull it from my holster. Without a sound, I take a deep breath and push my way through the open door, peering into the shadows. Nothing moves, but that doesn't mean he's not still here. I scan every inch of what's in front of me. It's silent.

The bathroom. Blair had said she locked herself in the upstairs bathroom.

I glance up the stairs, a part of me wanting more than anything to bolt up them to make sure she's okay, but that's not the right move yet. Right now, I need to clear the house and make sure the intruder's gone.

My heavy boots crunch on glass on my way down the hall. A picture frame from the looks of it, but the only thing I have to go on is the light from the moon, and a random streetlight pouring in through the large antique windows.

The house is large, but it doesn't take long for me to ensure the first floor is deserted. I slowly ascend the stairs, and the image of Blair curled up in the bathroom, terrified for her own life, flashes through my mind. My ears strain for the tiniest of sounds, but the only thing I hear is the pounding of my heart.

The upper hall is dark, except for the light pouring out of one room, and from beneath the door of another. I check the dark rooms first, but they're all empty.

I approach the light-filled bedroom and find myself in a space that screams femininity. It screams Blair. Pale green walls and white furniture are accented by flowers and framed photos. A small pile of clothes lay crumpled on the floor beside the bed, and the closet door stands wide open.

There's nobody here. He's gone.

Desperate to see her, to reassure myself she's all right, I turn from the room and approach the door with the light streaming from underneath. My heart thunders, and the only thing that'll calm it is seeing Blair.

With more force than I intend, I pound on the door. "Blair, it's me. Open up."

Her muffled sob comes from inside the closed-off room, and the sound grates at my heart. How any fucker could have hurt this woman is beyond me. I hate she's so afraid. I hate she can't even be safe in her own house. But she will be. I'll make sure she will be.

"Blair, darlin', please open the door. It's safe now."

The lock mechanism makes a clicking sound when she turns it from the other side, and then, there she is, her face streaked with tears. Her cat's clutched in her arms, even though the damn thing looks downright scary with its ears pressed flat against its head, growling a warning at me.

"Oh, God," she cries, dropping the cat to the ground and rushing into my arms. "I was so scared. I called the police, but—"

"Sssshhh," I tell her, hugging her tight. *Thank God she's unharmed.* "It's okay now, Red." She sobs against my shoulder, her wet tears soaking into my shirt. I continue to hold her as guilt works its way in for loving how her body feels pressed against mine in a situation like this. She pulls away from my shoulder and stares up at me with the most beautiful pair of green eyes I've ever seen. I take her face in my hands, wiping her tears away with my thumbs.

"Thank you," she whispers. "I didn't know what else to do."

"I gave you my number for a reason, sweetheart. I'm glad you used it."

She steps away from my grasp, and it takes every ounce of control I have to not audibly groan when she does. That thin towel's hiding fucking nothing.

"Me too," she admits, her gaze scanning the room with tears still in her eyes, her body trembling with fear.

The fucker ransacked her room when she was just a few feet away. Murderous fury prickles inside of me, thinking about how unprotected she is here on her own. That's going to change, right here and now.

"Get dressed."

Confusion flashes through her eyes. "What? But… I don't have anywhere else to go," she shutters.

"Bullshit. You're coming home with me, Red."

"I can't do that. We barely know each other."

I've stormed the castle twice to save her life. Formalities be damned.

"The hell you can't. I'm not leaving you here like a sitting duck."

"The cops—" she starts, before I cut her off.

"The cops didn't show, I did. You're safer with me. I can protect you, they can't," I growl.

She chews on her bottom lip. I don't want to push her, but the boys in blue will be here any minute. It would be better if neither of us were here, especially me.

"Okay," she agrees. She bends down to grab a few things from the pile on the floor. "Can you turn around so I can get dressed?"

Fuck. Does everything about this woman have be so fucking cute?

"Please," she pleads.

The sounds of sirens a few miles away call out in the quiet campus air. We've got five minutes tops before they show up here. We don't have time.

"We need to go, sweetheart. Don't worry about your stuff. I'll come back to get it once I know you're safe."

I spy a black hoodie near my feet and bend down to scoop it up.

"Here," I tell her. "Put this on." Slipping it over her shoulders, she zips it up.

"Let's go." Reaching out for her, she recoils.

"I can't leave without Jinx," she protests.

"Who the fuck is Jinx?"

"My cat."

Fucking great. Walter's going to lose his shit over a new four-legged roommate. He was just getting used to people again after his stint with the dog fighting ring. I haven't had a chance to test out other animals.

"Fine," I groan. "But we've got to hurry."

She bolts from the bedroom, back into the bathroom. She comes back a minute later with a hissing, moving lump inside of her zipped up hoodie. I shake my head at the sight.

"Grab those flip flops by the door," I tell her. "There's broken glass down there. I don't want you cutting your feet."

She does, and as soon as she's situated—minus the fact that she's still in a towel—I grab her by the hand and lead her down the stairs. The lights of the incoming cruisers illuminate parts of the first floor. We've got to hustle.

By the time we get outside, I nearly drag her down to the alley where I parked my bike, when police cruisers fly past the gravel entrance behind us.

"Get on," I demand while I swing my leg over the seat and flip the ignition. She slides on behind me with her squirming cat between us. "Hold on."

Popping the kickstand, I peel off toward home, with the claws of her cat digging into my back from inside of her jacket the entire way.

BLAIR

ONCE WE ARRIVED at GP's house, he shoved me inside and was gone, leaving me with an order to not step foot out of his house, and to not open the door off the kitchen until he got back. I watched from the front door as he mounted his bike again, and pulled out of the driveway.

The longer I wait for him to come back, the more I find myself examining my surroundings. His home is older construction, with some of the same features as mine. Vaulted ceilings. Crown molding. It even has the expansion archway from the entryway into the mail receiving area that was common back when this type of home was built. I pad through the first floor, finding several closed rooms off the main living space. A stark contrast to the open feel of my house. Oddly, all the rooms are empty, except for the kitchen on the back end of the first floor. Drop cloths and construction materials lay strewn all over the place. Is he remodeling it?

The strange thing is, his house feels oddly familiar. I don't remember ever being in this particular home, but Grandmother did have a tendency to visit all her neighbors with freshly baked goodies when the occasion arose. Southern hospitality and all. But I don't remember coming here on one of those trips. I think I would've remembered one so similar to ours. Maybe my house was built by the same builder? I shake the notion from my head. There's no way.

I get lost looking around his house, but then Jinx bites me a few times. Unzipping my hoodie to let her out, she goes ballistic, running across every corner of the house, and knocking over a stack of old boxes in the entryway.

"Dammit, Jinx," I curse. "We're guests here. Stop wrecking the place." She skids off up the stairs to hide. Finding her is going to be a pain in the ass later, but I'm not about to go upstairs without GP here. It's bad enough I was snooping around the first floor. Expanding my snooping to the second floor is where I'm drawing the line.

As I start to pick up Jinx's mess, my phone rings from inside my pocket.

"Shit," I swear when the detective's name flashes across the screen.

"Hello?" I mutter when I answer.

"Where the hell are you?" he yells into the receiver. "My officer's combed your house, and you're nowhere to be found."

"I'm at a friend's house," I lie. GP is a sort of a friend... I think. "I couldn't stay there."

"And is this friend the man you've been lying to me about?"

"No," I answer casually, continuing to disguise my lie. "A friend from school."

"I see," he fires back, suspicion clear in his voice.

I guess I'm not as good of a liar as I thought.

"It was my understanding that you were in the house when you called."

"I was, but if I'd stayed there any longer, I would've been dead, no thanks to you."

"My officers are not at your beck and call, Miss Thompson. You're not our only case."

"No kidding," I mutter under my breath.

"I'm going to ignore that jab, and hopefully, our suspect will have left us a little more to go on this time. My officers are processing the scene now. I'd advise you to stay at your friend's house for the time being."

"Okay..." GP didn't exactly give me a deadline on how long I could stay here in our short conversation. Not that staying at his house longer than tonight is a viable option at this point. I could reach out to Lindsey since she offered to help me earlier.

"I'll be in touch with what we find. You and your friend should stay in town."

"Where would I go, exactly?"

"With a friend like him, you could disappear like smoke on the wind, Miss Thompson."

Before I can ask him anything else, like coming to get my stuff while the cops are still there, he hangs up on me. *I'm guessing that's a no.*

I stalk over to the toppled boxes and begin scooping the contents back inside until one particular item draws my attention under the nearby end table. I get onto all fours to retrieve it, nearly hitting my head in the process.

Curiosity gets the best of me when I pull out a dusty, folded up photograph. *What the hell?* The older woman in the visible side of the image is my grandmother, in her favorite summer dress, with one of her fancy hats—as I called them—that she only wore on special occasions. Grandmother was the epitome of the Old South. Manners and hospitality were one of the biggest things she stressed to me growing up.

My finger traces over her image, missing her more now than ever.

I straighten the crease of the picture, and my stomach drops. To the left of Grandmother is a woman I don't recognize, and two young children in front of them both. One of them is me.

"What the hell?" I mutter in shock. *How did he get this photo?*

The front door swings wide open, and GP steps inside. I freeze. He stares down at me and the toppled box with a scowl.

"I leave you alone for ten minutes and you go through my shit?" he angrily questions.

I slide up from the floor to my feet, clutching the photo in my hand, and stomp to his spot by the door. "Why the fuck do you have a picture of me?"

He's taken aback by my question, confusion clear as day washing over his face.

"I don't," he fires back.

"Bullshit. Take a look for yourself." I shove the photo into his hand.

He looks down at it. "All I see here is a picture of me and my grandmother. I don't know the other two."

I step over to his side and examine it again. "No, that's me," I say, pointing to myself as a kid. "This is *my* grandmother." Seeing her smiling face sends a mournful pang to my heart.

"That's you?"

"Why would I lie about something like that? Yes, that's me."

"That's me." He points to the boy standing next to me in the photo with a huge grin on his face, one mirroring my own.

"That's not possible." I snatch the photo from him and look again. *This really happened.* I turn the image over and search for an inscription on the back, but there's nothing written.

"This says otherwise," he teases, leaning closer into my body.

I try to ignore his closeness, but it's calming to be near him. "How old were you here?"

He takes the photo out of my hand and studies it more carefully. "Maybe six or seven? I spent every summer with my grandmother before I started school back in Seattle, where I lived with my mom."

"That's about how old I was when my parents dropped me off on her doorstep with a bag of clothes, and without a goodbye."

His lips curl into a frown.

"Don't look at me like that. It is what it is. Not everyone lives in a fairy tale growing up. I just can't believe we knew each other as kids."

"Same. You'd think I'd remember playing with a pretty girl like you."

A warm blush flourishes over my cheeks.

"What?" he asks.

"No one's ever called me pretty before," I admit.

Putting his arm over my shoulders, he pulls me against his body. "They must've been blind, Red."

Silence falls between us, but it's soon disturbed by

the sound of something upstairs crashing to the floor. GP glances up to where the noise came from.

"Jinx may have run upstairs when I let her out," I explain, trying to play it off that my cat wasn't likely destroying his second floor in a fit of angry payback.

Smiling, he shakes his head. "Come on. I have someone you gotta meet."

GREENPEACE

I LEAD Blair to the kitchen, thinking of every unsexy thing I can to take my mind off the fact that she's still wearing nothing but a towel and a hoodie. Her legs are so goddamn long.

Just thinking about those legs wrapped around me has my cock straining against my fly. Fuck. bringing her back to my place may not have been the best idea.

Dog shit. Road kill. Fat Eddie down at the strip joint. The clubhouse toilet after it overflows thanks to Karma and hour-long shit sessions.

I clear my throat and pause outside the door. "So, you remember I told you I had a dog, right?"

Blair's face lights up with a smile, and she nods. *Fuck, she's beautiful.*

I place my hand on the door, trying to focus. "His

name's Walter, but I have to warn you, he's… a little scary."

Blair rolls her eyes and shoves at my arm playfully. "Just open the door, worrywart. I want to meet the boy that saved my life."

I gape at her for a moment, surprised at her eagerness. "Okay. But don't say I didn't warn you."

I push open the door, and there Walter stands, his head held high, his tail wagging up a storm. His tongue hangs out of his mouth as he grins up at us.

"Oh, my God," Blair squeals, pushing past me and into the room.

I reach for her, ready to warn her that Walter isn't much of a people person, but it's too late. She's already folded herself onto the floor next to him, nuzzling her face against his cheek.

"Hello, gorgeous boy," she coos. "So you're the boy who saved my life. Not only handsome, but brave."

I can't move. Never before have I entered the room with an unfamiliar person and not found Walter cowering in a corner, his lips pulled back from his teeth in a way that warns all of us to stay the fuck back.

I've never seen Walter nuzzle anyone, including myself. He's not one to show affection toward humans after the way he was treated by them.

Blair peers up at me from her place on the floor,

where she embraces my dog like he's a goddamned teddy bear, and grins. "He's amazing."

Her words snap me out of my state of shock, and I can't help but smile back. "He is," I admit. "Old Walter here's been through a lot, but he's a good boy... most of the time."

Blair continues scratching under his chin. "Oh, he's full of it," she tells Walter. "I bet you're a good boy all the time, aren't you?"

Walter presses himself closer to her, nearly knocking her back onto the floor. His way of agreeing with her, I assume.

A crash comes from upstairs. Walter stills, and Blair's eyes widen. "Jinx," she whispers.

I'd forgotten all about her crazy cat wreaking havoc on my second floor.

She stands and motions to Walter. "Will he be...?"

"I don't know." Before I have a chance to say anything, Walter darts past me, his feet pounding up the stairs before we even get out of the kitchen.

"Jinx!" Blair cries out, fear clear in her voice.

We hit the staircase. A single bark, and the sounds of a pissed off kitty, assault our ears from above.

"Walter, no!" I yell, my feet not moving fast enough for me to do anything about what's happening up there.

I reach the landing, and the sight before me stops me dead in my tracks. There in the corner of the hallway is

Blair's cat, her back pressed against the wall, her paw pressed on Walter's snout. Walter lays completely still, other than the wagging tail, and allows the insane feline to believe she's holding his head to the floor.

"Jinxy," Blair chides, brushing past me and scooping up her cat. "We're guests in this house. You don't treat your hosts this way."

Jinx purrs menacingly, her tail twitching with anger.

"Did she hurt you, handsome?" she asks Walter, her hand running along the top of his head. This is likely the most love, in this moment, he's ever experienced in his short life.

I watch the spectacle before me. *How the hell did we go from Blair holed up in the bathroom, hiding from her assailant, to both of us standing in the hallway of my grandmother's old house, trying to keep her cat from beating the shit out of my enormous dog?*

"Looks like your cat's the one we need to worry about," I finally say, still amazed by the turn of events, as well as the complete change in Walter's demeanor. My eyes wander to where her towel is slightly open above the knees. "Why don't we get you something to wear?"

She looks away from the animals, and for the first time, seems to realize just how little she's wearing. "That might be a good idea," she giggles. Her cheeks turn a shade of pink, making my mind go to a million different naughty places.

I turn and stalk toward my bedroom. *Bird shit. Hair balls. That dead possum Judge ran over last week.*

"Even just a T-shirt to sleep in," she says from behind me. "And the nearest couch, and a pillow. After tonight, I need some sleep."

I enter my bedroom, open a drawer, and pull out my favorite T-shirt. A well-worn Metallica shirt I got at one of the first concerts I ever attended. "Here," I say, tossing it at her. "And you will not be sleeping on a fucking couch. You take the bed."

She motions with a finger for me to turn around, so I do. Fabric rustles behind me, and all I can think about is her changing her clothes just a few feet away. *Shower grime. The smell of manure. Moldy bread.*

"I'm done."

Jesus, she looks fucking incredible. The soft grey material covers her like a dress, coming down to just above her knees. Her breasts come to full peaks, leaving little to my imagination. And my imagination is in full swing right now.

I point to the bed. "You sleep here, I'll take the couch. Tomorrow, we'll get you some clothes and make a plan."

Blair nods, her eyes wide.

I watch her, my heart pounding with every step she takes closer to me.

"Thank you, GP."

"Anytime, Red," I reply, my voice hoarse.

Her eyes never leave mine, and she presses her tiny hand to my chest as she pops up on her toes. Her lips graze against my cheek, and I'm enveloped in her sweet smell—wildflowers and rain.

When I'm not sure I can take it anymore, I clear my throat and take a step back. "I'll be downstairs if you need anything. Come on, Walter."

Walter glares at me before jumping up onto the bed and making himself comfortable.

"Walter!"

He doesn't move.

"He's fine," Blair says, pulling back the blankets, while Jinx curls up on a pillow. Walter's gaze is clearly telling me to get lost.

Fucking traitor.

"Good night, Blair." I pull the door closed behind me.

Chapter 15

BLAIR

GP'S SCENT, lingering on the pillows and sheets, wrapped me in a blanket of comfort from the second my head hit the pillow. It felt a bit dirty being in his bed while he took that tiny couch. His bed felt almost too big for me to be in alone, but Walter made up for it. Most of the night, he was plopped between my legs, with Jinx's tiny body draped across my head like a hat to be the farthest away from the beast who is still snoring from his claimed position.

Waking up in a strange man's bed, wearing nothing but his T-shirt, shouldn't be that odd on a college campus, but it is for me. Though, could I really classify GP as a stranger at this point?

My college aspirations were less about the experiences and more about the education, not "tasting freedom" for the first time as an adult.

I stir, and Walter's one good eye slightly opens into a slit, keeping watch on me, just like GP. I didn't miss him pacing outside my door more than a few times last night before exhaustion well and truly took me under. It was an odd comfort knowing he was still watching out for me, even in the safety of his own home.

"Good morning." I smile at Walter, giving him a rub on his head.

He leans into my touch with a groan. Jinx interrupts us, taking a swipe at him. Walter doesn't pay her a lick of attention and crawls up farther, almost lying on my belly.

"I can pet another animal, you know," I correct her with a soft *boop* to her nose.

Jinx looks over at Walter's even closer position and hisses at him. Walter pushes her with his nose, causing Jinx to spill over the edge of the bed and onto the floor. Landing on all fours, she just stares back at me, and I know I'll be paying for that slight in one way or another soon. I don't know when, but she'll get her revenge. Light on her feet, she walks over to the now cracked door and slips outside. The door nudges open wider, and the most heavenly smell of bacon wafts into the room. My stomach growls almost instantly once my feet hit the wooden floor.

"You smell it too, huh, Walter?"

Walter stretches, then hops off the bed. He stops by the door like he's waiting on me.

"I'm coming, buddy," I say, petting his head when I walk past him.

Walter and I descend the curved stairs to the first floor. In the kitchen, GP stands at the stove with his naked back to me. The leather vest he'd worn both times I'd been in his presence is gone. He never told me about his affiliation with a motorcycle club, but live around this town long enough, you'll be able to recognize the Black Hoods logo without a second glance. He looks oddly normal with it draped across his back.

Though, I have to admit, I like the view in front of me right now too—his muscular build, and the numerous tattoos on full display—but it's the jeans riding low on his hips as he dances to the rock music playing from his phone that almost takes my breath away. All I can do is stare. I knew he was built, but there isn't a word in the dictionary to explain this. Not a single one.

He smiles at me. "Morning."

"Uh, smorning," I blurt out. The second it leaves my lips, I want to crawl in a hole and die of embarrassment. *Smorning? Smooth, Blair. Real smooth.*

GP turns back to the pancakes, but I catch him laughing.

"Something funny?"

He returns his gaze to mine, and points to the top of my head with the spatula. "I like your bedhead, Red."

I reach up to feel it, and for the second time in a matter of minutes, that proverbial embarrassment hidey hole seems like a pretty good place to call home.

"Uh… I'll be right back," I mutter, then fly past him and into the bathroom off the kitchen where Walter and I met last night. In the corner of the room, I spy a cardboard box lid filled with shredded paper. A makeshift litter box. That definitely wasn't there last night.

I take a long look at my reflection in the mirror. "Shit." My red curls look like they decided today would be a great day to go rogue and take on the appearance of what you'd expect to see if I'd put my finger in a light socket. I try to fix it the best I can with some water from the faucet, but any more, and I'll look like a drowned, redheaded rat.

"Could this get any worse?" *Shit. I shouldn't have said that.*

With a deep breath, I muster up what's left of my dignity and return to the kitchen, just in time for GP to set down a large platter of pancakes, scrambled eggs, and bacon.

"Hope you're hungry," he declares, with a hint of nervousness in his voice. "I didn't think to ask if you like this kind of stuff. I have some canned fruit in the pantry if you don't eat meat."

"This looks delicious." I smile back. GP pulls out one of the dining chairs, and waits for me to sit down.

He leans in when he helps me scoot closer to the table, and I take in his scent—summer rain and leather, just like his sheets. Dammit. He smells and looks way too good to have me in his house. He takes the chair next to me and piles my plate high with everything on the platter. My stomach growls again when he sits it down in front of me.

"Thank you," I tell him, remembering my manners. "Did you make Jinx a litter box?"

"It's not much, but I'll pick her up one later."

"You don't have to do that. She has one already. She can just use it when we go home later."

His lips thin, but Walter bulldozes his way under the table, parking himself between my feet, and shoving his head into my lap.

"Go lay down," GP commands sternly.

"It's okay," I assure him. "I'm used to it. Jinx is a world class food stealer."

"So is he. Asshole stole an entire pizza off the counter a few days ago."

"He was hungry," I coo to Walter, slipping him a piece of crispy bacon under the table.

"Keep that up, he'll never let you leave." His teasing smile fades. "About that… I think it would be a good idea for you to stay here awhile."

"Are you inviting me to move in?"

He stills mid-bite.

"I really appreciate the offer, but I can't do that to you. I've already stolen your bed for one night. I can't do that again."

"You didn't steal my bed, I gave it to you. And you're far safer here, with me, than you are in that giant old house by yourself." His words say he's trying to reason with me, but the hard look in his eyes tells me he's not going to back down. This isn't an offer—it's a demand, one that sends a fiery bolt of arousal zinging straight between my legs.

"It is a comfy bed," I tease.

This time, GP chokes on his food.

"Best night's sleep I've had in a while, even with Walter sleeping between my legs." I don't miss the glare GP sends Walter's way.

"Think about it. It would make me feel better if you stayed here. It's not like I don't have the room."

"I was actually curious about that. Why is this place so empty?"

He grins. "So you were snooping around."

"No. I was acclimating myself because my host left as soon as we got here."

"First of all, I was checking the alley to make sure we weren't followed," he chides. "And going back to your snooping, I'm remodeling the house."

"To sell it?" Turn of the century houses like this were in demand. Not for their architecture, but for the large plots of land they occupied so close to campus. This neighborhood is the last one with original houses left.

"Not sure yet." He shrugs. "I figure I'd start with a remodel and see where things end up."

"It's a beautiful place. I'd hate to see another one fall to developers and student housing."

"The neighbors might just be enough to keep me here." He smiles, giving me a wink. "All finished?"

"I couldn't eat another bite." Wiping my face off with a napkin, I place it on top of the now empty plate. I have to admit, I didn't peg GP for the cooking type, but if breakfast was any indication, there's a lot more to him than meets the eye.

"If you want to get cleaned up, I put out some towels in my bathroom upstairs. I think the cops cleared out of your place this morning. We might be able to get in there and get your stuff."

"My clothes would be nice. Not that I don't appreciate your T-shirt."

His eyes trail up my body. Maybe I shouldn't have brought attention to the fact that the only thing between us is a thin piece of material.

"We could head over there later if you'd like."

"Could we do it after I get out of class? Today's supposed to be my first day as a TA."

"A what?"

"I'm a teacher's assistant in my doctoral program."

Arching his brow, he asks, "What are you studying?"

"Psychology."

"Didn't expect you to say that." He turns from the sink, leans against it, and crosses his arms over his broad chest. "Why psychology?"

"I want to help people." I shrug. "Helping someone through a mental health crisis is like a puzzle. You have to piece together how they tick first before you can help them fix it. Weird, I know, but I've always had an affinity for it."

"I can tell. You light up when you talk about it. That's why you were snooping around, isn't it? You were trying to figure me out."

"For the last time, I wasn't snooping around," I protest. "Jinx knocked that box over."

"Sure, Red. Blame it on the devil cat," he teases back, smiling wide. "What time is your class?"

"Ten thirty."

Glancing at his phone on the counter, he laughs.

"Why are you laughing?"

He doesn't answer me.

"What time is it? My phone kinda died in the middle of the night."

"Five after ten."

"Shit! I won't even make it there even if I run!"

"Relax, Red. I can get you there in ten minutes."

"You want to take me to class?" My eyebrow arches at the prospect. Riding on his bike to class might turn a few heads, but not in the way I want. I have enough attention on me as it is with the attack. Being seen with a Black Hood would just draw more ire and rumors from my classmates.

"I'm a full-service savior. What can I say?"

"I don't have any of my clothes," I fire back as an excuse, gesturing to his shirt. "This doesn't exactly fit the dress code."

He takes a long, lingering gaze up and down my body. It should make me feel uneasy, but it doesn't. "There's a box up in my room with some of my grandmother's old clothes from the attic. I was going to donate them, but you're about her size. Feel free to take what you want. I washed them, so they're clean."

Shit, he's got me cornered now. I want to refuse him, but if I don't take him up on his offer, I'll miss half of my first day as TA. It's a double-edged sword. Take the chance of starting more rumors, or make a good first impression with the professor.

"Are you sure?" Last chance. Please change your mind.

"If you keep asking me questions, you really will be late, Red. Go on."

Dammit. Rumors, it is.

I bolt from the kitchen and back upstairs to his room. Sure enough, a box full of old clothes sits in the corner. I rummage through them until I spot something that might work. It's a fitted red and white gingham dress. Not exactly my style, but without making a side trip home, only making me more late, I don't really have a choice. Pulling GP's T-shirt over my head, I slip on the dress.

The bodice is thick enough that going without a bra won't be that noticeable. I just wish I had panties. I turn to leave the room, and an idea hits me. GP's dresser might just hold the answer. I walk over, quietly open it, and find a pair of his boxers in the top drawer.

"This is so wrong," I mutter to myself as I slip them on, pulling them up over my hips and under the dress's belted waist. They're way too big, but you work with what you have. With luck, the belt will keep them in place so I don't manage to flash everything to the world —and GP.

"You coming or what?" he shouts from downstairs.

"Coming!" I yell back. I make it down to the bottom of the steps without him noticing I've stolen his boxers, but with the way he's staring at me, I'm not so sure.

He doesn't move when I walk past him toward the door.

"Are we going?" I ask.

"Shit, sorry. Yeah, let's go," he growls.

He follows me out the door, mumbling something about roadkill under his breath as we walk toward his bike, parked next to the house in the alleyway. He slides over the big black tank and fires up the engine, then motions for me to get on the back.

"Hold on tight," he reminds me, and I settle in. Wrapping my arms around his waist, I hang on for dear life when he peels out of the driveway, heading toward campus.

Chapter 16

GREENPEACE

THE PSYCHOLOGY DEPARTMENT at the university takes up a handful of blocks of the sprawling campus. Each building stands dreary and proud, surrounded by bespectacled students in ties and skirts, running to and from with stacks of books clutched in their hands. I follow Blair's finger pointing over my shoulder to a building just ahead.

Pulling to a stop in front of one of the larger buildings, I turn off the motorcycle, fully aware of the eyes on us. I couldn't care less. Let them see Blair on the back on my ride. That oughta scare off anyone looking to move in on her.

She shifts behind me, and instantly, I miss the heat of her soft body pressed against my back. I reach to take her hand, and she slips over the side, righting herself so that both feet are on the ground beside me.

"Thanks for the ride."

Her cheeks are flushed a hot shade of red. I don't know if they're like that from the ride itself, or from her classmates, who are all standing around watching us right now. Whatever it is, it's making my cock hard.

"What time you done?"

Her brow furrows. "Uh…"

"Simple question, Red. What time are you done?"

She glances around nervously, tucking a stray lock of curls behind her ear. "Um, three thirty today."

"Same building?"

Blair gapes at me and nods, her eyes wide. Her lips are parted, and she looks so damn cute, I can't stop myself. I lean in and brush my lips against hers. "See you then, darlin'."

"But—"

I can already imagine the protests she's about to spew at me, so I reach for the key and spark up my ride. Without another word, I wink at her and pull away. I can't hide my grin. *She's probably so damn annoyed with me right now.*

At the edge of campus, I shove all thoughts of Blair out of my mind, needing to get my head in the game. Thanks to some fancy computer searching by my buddy, Hashtag, we finally have a location on Kenny Dwyer, the man Carson said could tell us about the new dog fighting ring.

Near the gas station on the corner of Fifth and Wallace, I spot Karma and Stone Face standing beside their motorcycles at the edge of the parking lot. It's hard not to see them. Karma's the enforcer for the Black Hoods MC for a reason. The dude's absolutely massive. They don't call him Karma for no reason.

The same can be said for Stone Face. I've known him for going on eight years now, and I've never seen the man smile. And as for size, he has a good three inches on Karma, and probably thirty pounds of muscle more.

There's a reason Judge sent these two to accompany me on this little expedition. Nobody can wrangle an answer from an unwilling man like Karma or Stone Face. The sight of them alone is intimidating. Top that off with them already pissed about the dog fights, they'll have Kenny Dwyer pissing in his pants.

""'Bout fuckin' time," Karma drawls when I pull into the empty space beside them.

I glance at my watch and roll my eyes. "Chill your nuts, K. I said to meet me around ten."

"Around must mean something different to you."

Stone Face nods his greeting, and is already straddling the massive frame of his Harley, ready to go and bust some heads. He never has been much for banter, no matter how funny it might be.

Karma looks his way and chuckles. "Let's do this shit."

I rattle off the address I got from Hashtag, and as a unified trio, we head out onto the road and make the short trip to the junkyard at the edge of town. According to Hashtag, Dwyer's old man owns the yard, but has been too old and frail to run it for years. That job's fallen on his son's shoulders. Kenny took over, but not without bringing in a little extra cash on the side. Like using the yard to store and starve dogs to the point they're blind with rage, then thrown into a ring to tear each other's throats out.

Lucky for us, but not so lucky for Kenny, someone left the front gate of the yard open, giving us free access to ride right into the center of it. Kenny himself stands dead center in a wide opening, surrounded by mounds of scrap metal and rusting appliances.

He watches us pull up to him with wide eyes, and I can practically read his mind. He's likely trying to decide whether to stand his ground or run like hell. Yet again, lucky for us, Kenny's a dumbass, and chooses the first option.

Our motorcycles fall silent. "Kenny Dwyer?" I ask.

He gapes back at me, his stance wider than before, his shoulders held firm. An attempt to make himself appear more intimidating. *Nice try, asshole.*

"Who wants to know?"

Stone Face takes a few steps toward him. "I do."

Staring up at the giant before him, all the color drains

from his face. His Adam's apple bobs when he gulps, but he doesn't reply.

"You might want to answer the question," Karma advises, peering around Stone Face's back. "My buddy here doesn't like to be ignored."

Kenny rips his eyes from Stone Face and flicks them toward Karma, and then to me. "What do the Black Hoods want with Kenny Dwyer?"

This fucking guy must think we haven't done our homework. I've seen his photo—we all have. Unless Kenny has a twin—and for the record, we know that he doesn't—there isn't a doubt in any of our minds who's standing before us.

Before I even get a chance to reply, Kenny's on his knees, his face twisted in pain. His head's tilted toward the sky, thanks to the meaty fist embedded in his hair, yanking it to the point he might just be bald after this little encounter.

"Where are the fucking Anderson brothers?" Just like Stone Face. Short, to the point, and laced with an indescribable amount of pain.

"I don't know what you're—Ahhh!" Kenny's hands fly up, covering Stone Face's in a desperate attempt to pull them from his hair. "Stop! Fuck!"

Karma lights a cigarette and leans against his motorcycle, clearly settling in for a show. "I'd answer the man," he says with a smirk. "Once he gets started, it's hard as fuck to rein him in."

"I don't know anything!" he cries. "Fuck! Let go of my fucking hair."

I take a step forward, and Stone Face does me a favor by yanking Kenny's hair in such a way, he can't help but look right at me. "See, I happen to know you're lying, Kenny, and I don't like being lied to." I point to Karma. "And Karma over there? He definitely doesn't like being lied to."

Tears of anger and defeat stream down Kenny's face.

"What about you, Stone Face?" I ask, keeping my voice calm and casual. "You like being lied to?"

Stone Face gets down real low, his lips right beside Kenny's ear. I don't know what he says to him in that moment, but Kenny's hands drop. His face becomes the palest shade of white a man could ever be, and I can practically see the defiance leave him.

"I don't know where they are," he confesses.

Stone Face pulls back a fist.

Kenny's hands shoot up into the air. "Wait! I–I d– don't know where they are right now, but I know where they'll be in a few days. I know where the fight's going to be."

Stone Face drops his fist, and I squat down in front of Kenny so we're practically nose to nose. "Tell me."

"The old pig farm on I-84, down near the county line."

I glance back at Karma, and he nods. Glad someone knows what the fuck he's talking about.

"Friday night at nine fifteen. That's when it starts."

"There a password?" Karma asks.

"I don't fucking know—Ahhh! Motherfucker!"

Stone Face smirks a little as he twists harder. He loves this shit.

"Machete!" Kenny cries. "The password is machete."

Karma rolls his eyes. "Real clever," he scoffs. "Let him go, Stone. We got what we need."

Stone Face shoves Kenny to the ground, his teeth mashing into the dirt. I watch him roll to his back and press his hands to the top of his head.

"You won't stop them," he warns, and it's clear he's happy about that.

"We shall see," I call from over my shoulder. And that's when I see him.

There, curled in the shade of a pile of old refrigerators, a brown and white pit bull lays. At least, I think that's what color he is. It's hard to tell, because the most dominant color on his coat right now is red. Blood.

The dog doesn't move. He doesn't whimper. He doesn't even look up at us. But he's alive—barely.

Before I even know what I'm doing, my fist crashes into Kenny Dwyer's face, and I can feel the crunch of bone beneath my knuckles. I hit him once, twice, then a third time. These fucking assholes. The pain they cause, just to gamble on the fight of two poor, innocent dogs is despicable. There's a special place in Hell for these people, and if I have anything to say about it, I'll help send them there.

Kenny doesn't try to fight back. I think I knocked him out with the first punch, but I don't even know. All I know is rage. Rage and desperation to stop this shit.

I've experienced firsthand how much damage these motherfuckers can do to a dog. I nursed Walter back to health myself. I slathered salve on his broken skin and iced his swollen joints. I took my time getting close to him, giving him every opportunity to trust a human for the first time in his short life.

Kenny Dwyer did that to him. The Anderson brothers did that to him. They caused that pain, and they caused that poor dog over there to spend his last moments of life curled up in agony in the center of a shitpit junkyard, alone and afraid.

"Okay! GP, stand down!" Karma's words. Yanking on my shoulder, he snaps me back to the present.

Kenny lies unconscious on the ground at my feet, his face nearly unrecognizable from the beating I just delivered. A couple of guys in coveralls stand out in the yard, their eyes on us, but make no move to do anything about it. Smart men.

And the dog. He's not in that spot on the grass anymore. He's been moved farther into the shade and onto the lap of a giant man. Stone Face cradles the broken dog like a baby, his voice low and soothing, his once violent hands now calming and gentle.

I don't move. I don't speak. Karma and I just stand there, quietly, watching as the most dangerous man we know provides a loving sendoff to a dog who has never known a moment of love or peace in his life.

BLAIR

STOP LOOKING AT THE CLOCK. *Don't do it.* I check again for what has to be the hundredth time in the last two hours. *Goddammit.*

I brush my hand across my face in frustration. Why can't I concentrate? This is one of my favorite subjects, but the second I try to listen to the lecture, my mind drifts back to this morning. I replay the conversation over and over again the longer I sit here. How GP looked when he didn't know I was watching him dance. His smile, and his deep laugh when he was teasing me. Even the way I felt with my arms folded around him while I sat on the back of his bike, the wind blowing through my hair on the drive to class. Everything about GP is both frustrating and comforting at the same time. My curse and my savior wrapped in a sexy enigma of a man.

"Miss Thompson?" the professor calls out to me,

snapping me back to reality. *Shit. What was he talking about again?*

"I'm sorry, Professor Brewer. I don't think I heard your question." More like, I hadn't heard a damn word he'd said since my ass hit the seat. *Thanks, GP.*

His weathered face scowls back at me. "Had you been listening, we were discussing the correlation of opioid addiction and deep state depression in young adults. You might consider getting your head out of the clouds and paying more attention. This will be on the first exam."

Could I make a worst first impression on not only the professor of one of the hardest courses I will take in this doctoral program, but the professor I'd be assisting over the summer until I receive my permanent assignment for the academic year this fall? If I could facepalm without anyone else noticing, mine would be a world record.

"I apologize, sir. Won't happen again."

"Be sure that it doesn't," he sternly growls before returning to his presentation. *Great.* That meeting after class to discuss my roles and responsibilities just got a lot more nerve-wracking.

The class drags on, and the longer the clock ticks slowly by, the bigger the urge I have to just go back home, crawl under the covers, and pray for a do-over. The worst part is, going home isn't even an option at this point. *Fuck my life.*

Professor Brewer finally finishes up his lecture a few minutes past the scheduled end of the class. The other students take off immediately from the classroom, leaving the two of us alone. I gather my things and head to the lecture bench with my proverbial tail between my legs.

Professor Brewer looks up as I approach. "Before you give me some sob story about your predicament, Miss Thompson, I want to make you aware that you volunteered to fill the temporary vacancy I had for my summer schedule. My expectation is that you pay attention, no matter what side of the lecture you sit on."

"I understand. I don't expect you to give me special accommodations, Professor."

"Good," he grumbles. "Unfortunately, I will be unable to meet with you to discuss your position as previously scheduled." He rummages around in his bag, retrieves a piece of paper, and thrusts it into my hands. "I took the liberty of typing up my expectations, and a tentative schedule."

I scan through the paper and hide my grimace. There, in plain black and white type, is a list of rules and responsibilities a mile long. I knew working for someone as tenured and respected as Professor Brewer would be difficult, but this is overkill. There goes my free time.

"Thank you," I force out, trying to conceal my displeasure.

"I'll see you first thing tomorrow morning, Miss Thompson," he mutters, grabbing his bag before walking past me. "Don't be late."

"I won't," I call out after him, but he's gone. Along with any chance of my perfect GPA staying that way.

Dejected, I walk out of the lecture hall, intent on trying to find a way to make amends with Professor Brewer tomorrow, and salvage our now damaged working relationship. Thanks to my inattentiveness, I smack hard against a nearly immovable object, which sends me crashing onto my ass with a thud.

"Shit!"

"Allow me to help you up," a smooth, accented voice says, extending a large hand out to help me to my feet.

"Thanks," I mutter, taking it, then righting myself. Dusting off my dress, I try to give myself a second to reassemble my ego before gazing up, only to realize the man is none other than Professor Daniel Coates. A world-renowned expert in the field of psychology, and the man whose work I've been following for the last several years. This man has literally redefined our field in the way we treat patients with bipolar depression, and I just bowled him over in the hallway. Could today possibly get any worse?

"I'm so sorry. I wasn't looking where I was going," I apologize profusely. "I should've been paying more attention."

"Tosh. It was nothing more than an accident." His British accent rolls over me, smooth as silk.

"Are you all right?"

"I'm fine," I admit. Physically, yes. My pride? Not so much. "I really am sorry about running over you like that, Professor Coates."

"Ah, so you know who I am, then," he surmises.

"Blair Thompson," I blurt out quickly. "I'm a big fan of your work, Professor."

"I'm pleased to make your acquaintance, Blair," he says, offering his hand.

I reach forward and shake his firmly.

"I hear you're assisting Brewer this summer. First day not go well?"

If he can read my expression, there's no doubt in my mind that I didn't hide it well from Professor Brewer. I couldn't have screwed up his first impression of me anymore than if I had streaked through the classroom mid-lecture.

"It was my fault. I was a bit distracted during the lecture, and he caught me off guard."

"I've been in a number of his lectures, my dear. It's not you. The man should have retired ages ago."

He's not wrong on that account, but I have no right to agree with him out loud—especially to one of his peers.

"I hate to see someone of your caliber—as I'm told by

Professor McCallen—waste their talent working for someone like him."

My advisor… and she'd talked about me? Why? She hadn't mentioned that to me at all. Why wouldn't she have said something?

"It's experience," I answer with a shrug. "It doesn't help that I missed the deadlines for the opportunities I really wanted to apply for." Namely *his* summer intern program. I was still pissed at myself for missing the deadline to apply to work for him, but seeing as I was in the hospital recovering, I had no other choice.

"I do hope you apply for the opening I have this fall, Miss Thompson. A bright mind like yours shouldn't be wasted in such a manner."

I try to hide the excitement dancing inside of me. A professor of his caliber shouldn't know anything about me. I'm a peon compared to him in the psychology world. Getting to his level of recognition and achievement was what my dreams were made of.

"I plan on it," I beam.

He smiles, and someone calls out to him from the other end of the hall. "I do have to get going, but please apply." He bids me goodbye, walks down the hallway, and glances back at me before disappearing into a room.

When he does, every single ounce of excitement pours from me at once, and I spin in a circle, squealing out loud. It would be the chance of a lifetime to work for

Professor Coates. An endorsement from a man like him, and I could have my pick of any job I want. My career trajectory could skyrocket in ways I've only ever imagined.

Maybe today isn't so bad after all.

The loud chime of the campus bell tower snaps me back to reality. *Shit!* GP is probably out there already waiting on me. I make my way out of the building toward the center parking lot. A few of the girls walking behind me spot GP before I do. Their coos about that sexy man and his bike make me roll my eyes.

I approach where he leans against his bike, with his arms crossed over his broad chest.

"You look happy," he says with a smile. "Professor must've gone easy on you for almost missing his class." He slides from his position and grabs a bright red helmet off the back of his bike. "Got you something today." He hands it to me, and it's not until he does that I notice his bloody hands.

"What happened to you?" I inquire, arching my brow.

He looks down at his battered knuckles, and wipes the blood off against his jeans. "It's nothing, Red."

"That's not nothing," I argue, grabbing his hand to inspect it closer. "This looks like you got into a fight with a brick wall."

"Maybe I did." He winks at me, but pulls his hands away.

What's he hiding from me? I'm not stupid. Any guy willing to charge head-first into a stranger's house to save her likely has some demons in his closet. But physical evidence like this means something happened. What did he do?

"You're sure you're all right?" I push harder.

"I'm fine, sweetheart. You hungry?"

He's deflecting. I guess the conversation about his hand is over. We'll see about that, though. Two can play this game, and I have all night to find out more.

"I could be," I admit with a shrug. "What do you have in mind?"

"You like barbecue?"

"As a Texan, it's kind of a requirement," I tease.

He throws his leg over his bike and pats the seat behind him. "Hop on, Red. We can swing by the store on the way home to grab what we need for dinner."

I start to get on the bike, but he stops me, pointing to the helmet in my hand. "Put it on."

"Do I have to wear this?" I protest.

"Don't like your present?"

"Fine," I concede. Affixing the helmet correctly, I click it into position. Lindsey steps out of one of the buildings on the other side of the lot and I wave to her, but she doesn't wave back. Weird, considering her offer to help just yesterday. Maybe she doesn't recognize me from this far away.

"Who are you waving at?" GP asks, his fingers on the key in the ignition.

"A friend," I declare. "How do I look?" I pivot on my heels, spinning around to model my new accessory.

"You look beautiful, Red. Matches your hair."

His comment makes me frown.

"What's wrong?'

"Just realized this is going to give me helmet hair."

"Someone could wreck us, and you're worried about helmet hair." He laughs hard. "The things that come out of that cute mouth of yours, Red."

"Don't laugh at me," I growl. I climb on his bike and wrap my arms around his firm, muscled waist. "You try combing through these curls with windblown helmet hair, and we'll see how you like it."

"If it's anything like your bedhead, we're definitely in trouble," he teases. He starts the engine and pops the kickstand. I can feel him laughing at me all the way to the grocery store.

GREENPEACE

PULLING the potatoes and steaks off the grill, I make my way back into the kitchen. Blair's at the counter, tossing a salad, a beer open in front of her. Her hips sway to the music from the radio, and her cat zigzags around her ankles while she works, clueless about anything going on other than the task at hand.

The woman is gorgeous. She's sweet and kind. Walter loves her. She also looks like she belongs in my kitchen, drinking the beer I bought for her, getting ready to eat the food I cooked.

What the fuck are you thinking, man? This is not the road to go down right now. Or ever, for that matter.

"Dinner's ready," I say, placing the food in the center of Grandmother's ancient, distressed dining table.

I watch her swig back her beer and scoop up the

salad to bring to the table, and a grin spreads across my face.

"Thank God," she groans. "I'm starving."

I pull out a chair, and motion for her to take a seat. Once she's settled, I sit next to her. The two of us set about making up our plates without a word, but the silence is broken when she lets out a moan that has every single drop of testosterone in my body on alert.

"Oh, God. I haven't had food from the grill in so long. This is delicious."

I clear my throat, and suddenly, I'm not so hungry anymore. *Anthills. Maggots. Wads of gum under my table at a restaurant. Fuck.* "Glad you like it."

My words are what a guy like me should say when he's cool, but I'm not feeling very cool right now. Blair places another bite between those full pink lips of hers and chews. Her eyes roll back, and she lets out yet another moan of pleasure.

Dog shit. Karma's hairy ass. The smell inside a truck stop bathroom.

"I can't believe we knew each other as little kids," she says between bites.

It takes serious effort for me to concentrate on her words and not her lips. *Jesus Christ, man. You need to get laid.*

"Yeah…" I answer, taking a bite of my own while looking down at the picture she put on the table across from us. "We weren't very old there, were we? I'd say I was maybe six."

Blair nods. "Yeah, I look about the same. We obviously spent some time together. I mean, there's photographic evidence of that. So why don't I remember you?"

I shrug. "I spent every summer up here with my grams."

She frowns. "Wait a minute… I do remember this one boy. He was mean to me all the time. He used to pull on my pigtails and make me cry."

A sudden memory flashes through my mind so fast, I can't quite catch it all.

"But his name was… Blake? No. Brad? No, it was Brock! I remember now. The kid I'm thinking of was named Brock. He was terrible."

I lay down my fork and turn to meet her gaze. Her red hair jogs yet another memory. The little red-haired girl used to come over with her grandma to play, but all she ever wanted to do was play house. She wanted me to be the dad and her to be the mom, and for us to have a "baby," played by this creepy doll she had, whose eyes closed every time you laid it down.

There's no way six-year-old me was going to pretend to be anyone's husband. I wanted to play hide and seek or build a fort. That little girl was a pain in the ass. And I remember tugging on those pretty, curly red pigtails just to get her to leave me alone.

"Holy fuck," I mutter.

"What?" She stares at me, her eyes filled with questions, still not quite putting two and two together.

I offer my hand to her. "Brock Fletcher, nice to meet you."

"No!" she gasps, her hand flying up to cover her mouth. "You mean, you're that awful little boy?"

I pretend to be offended. "I like to think I'm more of an awful big and scary man now."

Blair's hand falls from her face, and she gapes at me before throwing her head back, and howls with laughter. I can't help but join her. The whole thing is bizarre. What are the chances that she's the same kid I used to hate having over to this same house twenty years ago? That we'd actually spent time together when we were younger?

Our laughter fades, and Blair holds her belly, a single tear streaming down her face. She lets out a slow breath and giggles a little more. "You were an asshole," she informs me.

"I still am," I reply with a grin.

I don't expect it when her face grows serious. "You're my hero, though" she whispers.

Our eyes lock, and for a moment, I can't look away. *Her hero.* I've never been anyone's hero before, but if I was going to be anyone's, I'd want to be hers.

Knock that shit off, asshole. That's the least of your worries right now.

It takes effort, but my own self-admonishment is enough to make me force my eyes from hers. I grab my empty plate and stand, breaking the moment we were having. Passing her on my way to the sink, I see what can only be disappointment flash in her eyes.

Fuck.

Suddenly, what had once been a fun evening filled with laughter and great conversation has become awkward. From behind me, Blair pushes away from the table, and her chair scrapes across the floor.

I don't move when her footsteps approach, or when her shoulder brushes mine repeatedly while she rinses off her plate. I don't even move when she releases a subtle sigh before she turns to walk away.

"Ah, Walter," she mumbles. "You need some more water, buddy?"

I turn and watch her bend forward to pick the bowl up off the floor. A flash of dark blue peeks out from beneath the hem of her dress. A very familiar dark blue. I gape at her. *Nah. She wouldn't... would she?*

She moves to stand beside me, filling the bowl with water from the tap, but all I can think of is what she has on under that dress. Her scent surrounds me. Everything about her overwhelms me.

She's beautiful. She's intelligent. She's brave and

kind. She has a great sense of humor, and legs that stretch a mile long. Isn't she everything I've always wanted, but never dared to hope for?

I watch her bend forward again to place the water dish on the floor, and when the blue flashes from beneath her dress again, I snap.

Before I know it, I'm moving toward her. She turns, her eyes wide with surprise, but then they change. Fuck me, do they change. Alarm turns to need. A need I know all too fucking well, because I need her too, so fucking bad.

Taking her arm gently in my hand, I pull her forward until her chest is pressed to mine. "What are you wearing under that dress, Red?"

A wicked grin grows slowly on her face, and she stares at me with what could never be mistaken for anything but what it is—a challenge. "Guess."

My eyes fall closed, and I drop my head, burying my nose in the delicious place where her neck ends and her shoulder begins, drinking her in. She smells so fucking good. This time, I don't even bother trying to stop it. This time, there's nothing either one of us can do.

When her hand comes up and rests along the side of my cheek, I lift my head and meet her gaze. "I take it you like me in your underwear?"

My only answer is a growl. My lips crash onto hers, my heartbeat roaring so loud, the neighbors can probably hear it. She presses back, and her fingers twist into my hair, her kiss deep, her own need powering against my own.

"Tell me to stop," I mumble, moving my lips from her mouth to her neck. "Tell me to stop now, Red, or I won't be able to."

Her hands in my hair fist tighter, and her thigh wraps around my waist. "Don't you dare fucking stop."

With a growl, I reach down and lift her other thigh, cradling her sweet ass in my hands while she winds her legs around my waist. Her heat presses against my cock, straining at the confines of my jeans.

Her lips continue their glorious assault on mine as I make my way toward the stairs. She's so soft, so sweet, I almost decide to say fuck it, and just take her here on the creaky old steps. But I don't. She deserves more than that.

When we reach the bedroom, I lay her back on the bed, climbing between her legs. Her eyes gaze up at me, a soft smile on her lips. Her fingertips come up and graze along my cheek, sending a shiver down my spine. "You're so handsome."

"You're fucking gorgeous."

Her eyes flare with need, and in a move that would put a pro wrestler to shame, she has me on my back, and is climbing on top of me. Her lips are swollen from our kisses, and her cheeks are flushed as she yanks at my pants. "Take them off," she gasps.

She doesn't need to ask me twice. I lift my ass and kick them off. As soon as they hit the floor, I have her dress over her head and sailing through the air.

I can't move. She's perfect. Her breasts are creamy and full, her nipples begging for me to press tender kisses to each one. Her narrow waist widens out at the hips like an hourglass. My cock grows harder than it's ever been before.

I watch Blair's eyes widen.

She gazes down between her legs at the place where her core presses against my hardness. "It's been a long time," she admits. "A really long time."

"Take your time, Red. I'm in no hurry to get this over with."

When she lifts her hips and grasps my cock, the sight alone is enough to send me over the edge. I watch her position herself over top of me, and then slowly—so, so slowly—she takes me inside.

She's so tight. So warm. So fucking incredible.

I want to whip her around and fuck her. I want to plunge myself deep inside of her and revel in feeling her everywhere. But I don't. I let her take control, let her lead the race. I let her make love to me, her gaze never leaving mine. Her hands wrap around my wrists, and she brings my palms to her breasts, pressing them there, letting her head fall back.

Her hips swivel and sway, her body encapsulating me like a silk glove. Her hair swings, brushing against my balls. Her moans of ecstasy tells me she's so fucking close.

She's incredible. Every move she makes brings me closer and closer, and just when I think I can't hold it in for another second, she lets out a moan I'll never forget for as long as I walk this Earth.

Her pussy tightens around me, and I'm done. Any self-control I have disappears with the rippling of the walls of her pussy. I hold her close, giving her everything, pumping every ounce of pleasure I have into her.

When she's done, she drops her head to my shoulder and giggles. "Oh, my God," she says. "I'm so freaking sorry."

I'm still unable to breathe properly, but I respond anyway. "What could you possibly have to be sorry for?"

"I came so quick. I didn't mean to."

I lift her face so I can look in her eyes. "Baby, anytime you want to come on my cock, you can. And don't you ever apologize for it, because we're not done yet."

I whip her around and onto her back, eliciting a squeal of laughter. Grinning, I bring her nipple to my mouth. Silly girl. She thought it was over, but I'm just getting started.

Chapter 19

BLAIR

"DOES SHE ALWAYS DO THAT?" GP asks, looking at the headboard of his bed where Jinx is perched, watching over us.

"She's gargoyling." I laugh against his chest. "Just ignore her."

"I don't think I can do that," he huffs. "She's got this look on her face, like she's trying to figure out if she's going to eat me or let me live."

"Bless your heart," I say with a giggle. "Who'd have thought a big guy like you would be afraid of a little old cat."

His eyes remain on Jinx. "I'm not afraid, just overly cautious, seeing as how she went after Walter the other day. How long does she do this for?"

"Could be hours. Jinx kinda does whatever she wants, if you couldn't already tell."

Men. Walter can whine outside the door all he wants, but one little old cat watches them and it's game over. I shift away from GP's warm body, and gently shoo her off the headboard. She lands on the floor with a thud, and a growl of displeasure. "Happy now?"

"Yes," he laughs. "I don't have to worry about her trying to kick my ass for holding you." He pulls me back down atop his naked chest and snakes his arm around my shoulder, lazily brushing his fingers across it. "I like the way you feel against me like this."

His admission is a bit shocking, because I like it as well. If you'd have asked me if I thought in a million years I would wind up in bed with him, I'd have laughed in your face. This entire situation and relationship is far outside my comfort zone, but he makes me feel so different the longer he holds me.

"You still awake?' I tease him when quiet snores slip from his mouth.

"Why? You ready to go again, Red?" He stirs, planting a kiss against my forehead. Seeing him like this is a stark contrast from the way he is when he's storming the gates to protect me.

"Not that," I declare, making him frown. "We still need to go over to my house to get my stuff."

"You're right. As much as I would like to stay in this bed with you the rest of the night, we should get over there before it gets too late. Then, we can get back to more of this." He draws me into a kiss before throwing the blanket away and sliding out of the bed. His tight ass is on full display as he walks to his dresser, grabs a pair of basketball shorts from the drawer, and puts them on. The way they hang low over his hips makes me second guess going to get my stuff. It could wait. Right?

He turns back to me and grins. "Are you getting out of there, or do I need to get back in there and drag you out… later?"

"If we did that, I'd have to wear your boxers to class tomorrow," I fire back when I leave the bed to scrounge around for something to wear, since my borrowed dress isn't fit for the public anymore, thanks to GP. I just need something to get by until I have my own clothes, and risking another one of his grandmother's fashion classics isn't going to cut it. "You don't happen to have another one of your T-shirts I could borrow, do you? I seem to be without wearable clothing again."

Rummaging through his drawers, he pulls out another one of his shirts, and a second pair of athletic shorts, and tosses them to me. Slipping them on, I pull the drawstring tight around my waist. They're both way too big, but they'll do for a few more minutes. We head downstairs, and while I'm slipping on my flip-flops, Walter brushes up against my leg.

"Hey, buddy," I coo to him while scratching his ears. "Do you want to go with us?"

Walter grumbles happily, and heads straight for the door.

GP shakes his head at us. "He's got your number. You know that, right?"

"Think I care?" I chide him. "He's earned some extra attention if you ask me."

"Let's head out before Jinx convinces you to take her too." Opening the door for us, we step out into the cold night air. It doesn't take long to reach my house.

"Let me go in first." Holding up a hand, he peers at the giant old house. "I want to take a look around before I let you inside. Walter, stay with Red." Heading up the steps, he rips the crime scene tape away from the front door, and disappears into the house.

"Lord, I hope my stuff's still in there," I tell Walter, who chuffs softly in agreement.

I should've come over first thing this morning, but I didn't even think about the fact that the police wouldn't have the keys to lock the front door.

He's gone for several minutes before reappearing at the front door, waving for me to come in. Stepping back into my house after what happened makes it feel even more foreign. Thick layers of black powder cover everything inside. *Thanks for cleaning up, Detective Douchebag.*

"Coast is clear. Let's get what you need and get out of here." GP's body tenses as he scans every square inch of the house. "You head on upstairs. I'll stay down here and keep an eye out."

"Okay. Could you maybe get some of Jinx's things for me out of the laundry room? There's a spare litter box, food, and a bag of his treats in the cabinet above the washer."

"Anything else you need from down here? Cell phone charger, maybe?"

"That's upstairs, smarty-pants," I tell him with a grin. "I think that should be all for down here. Feel free to raid the pantry for anything you want to take over to your house. I hate that I'm eating all your food."

"Let's not worry about food. Just get the essentials, Red. I can handle the food budget just fine."

I leave him and Walter on the first floor and head up the stairs. Every hair on my body stands on end as I walk back into my bedroom. It feels so wrong here. I try to shake off the feeling of my attacker's invasion, and focus on getting what I need. Grabbing my biggest suitcase from the closet, I toss in a random assortment of clothes. Thankfully, my book bag with my purse and laptop still inside are on my dresser where I left them. Pulling the chargers for my laptop and phone from the sockets, I place them in the front pocket of my book bag, along with the photo of my grandmother from the nightstand.

"Clothes. Laptop. Purse. Book bag. Chargers. What else do I need?"

Toiletries. How could I forget those? I pad into the bathroom and grab everything out of the shower, as well as a few of my extras from the cabinet under the sink. This will definitely cover me for a few days until things cool down. I deposit all of it into my suitcase before zipping it up. I scan over my room one more time. *Shit. My delicates.*

"Good Lord, Blair," I chastise myself. "That's the first thing you should've gotten." Wearing GP's boxers got me into enough trouble earlier. A very sexy kind of trouble. Grinning at the memory, I step over to my dresser and yank open the top drawer. Looking down into it, my heart stutters. My chest won't move—suddenly heavy, like it's turned to stone. The drawer is empty. Every single pair of my panties are missing. The only thing inside is a slip of paper with a heavy script across it.

With a shaking hand, I reach out and pluck the paper from the empty drawer.

I'm still here, Blair. Tonight was not our night. But it's coming very soon, my love.

A scream spills from my lips, and I scramble away from the note, falling against my bed.

"Blair!" GP yells from downstairs. His heavy footfalls thud up the stairs, with Walter trailing right behind him. He runs right to me and pulls me into his arms. "What's wrong?"

I don't respond. I can't speak.

"Red, you're scaring me. Talk to me, sweetheart."

"T–The drawer," I stutter. "There's a note." My voice cracks as I struggle to tell him about my missing panties, but he lets me go, walks over to the open drawer, and pulls out the note.

"Motherfucker! He's a dead man, Blair. I'm going to fucking kill him!" he rages, kicking a pile of towels on the floor the angrier he gets. "He won't touch you as long as I'm breathing, I promise you that."

"He took all of my panties," I whisper. Walter presses his warm body against me, and I gape up at GP in shock. "He's been in my room."

"This is why you're staying with me. I can protect you." The intensity flaring in his eyes is unlike anything I've ever seen before. He means every word he's saying. He'd kill to protect me, a concept that should scare the ever-loving fuck out of me. But right now, it's the kind of protection I need. The only way I'm going to survive this is by his side.

"Get your stuff," he demands. "We need to leave, now."

I reach for my book bag, and GP grabs my suitcase. With my hand in his, he pulls me down the stairs behind him. Stopping at the bottom, he picks up the things for Jinx, putting them into my arms. "We're going to go out your back door and down the alley. Stay quiet."

"Why can't we take my car?"

"Blair, honey, I know you're scared, but your car can be tracked. It needs to stay here."

I hadn't thought about that, but he's right. If my car moved to another house, it would give away my location, like a beacon. "What about the front door? I need to lock it."

"Did that while you were upstairs. Come on. We need to get back to my place, where you'll be safe." Grabbing my hand again, and with Walter in tow, he leads us both out into the darkness, away from my house and to the safety of his. Yet, the question remains: would I be safe anywhere?

Chapter 20

GREENPEACE

I SCAN every shadow on the short walk back to my house, my body humming with rage at the note in Blair's drawer. How had the fucking cops not found that? When had the attacker even left it? This could mean he'd been back since last night.

My phone buzzes in my pocket, but between the suitcase, book bag, cat supplies, and the dog, my hands are fucking full. "Just around the corner," I tell her, even though she likely already knows that.

"Thank God," she gasps. Her hands are just as full as mine, and the walk home hasn't been leisurely. We hauled ass.

As soon as we step inside the warmly lit house, we drop all the bags and shake out our aching limbs.

"Would've been easier to take the car," Blair mutters, rolling her shoulders with a grimace of discomfort.

My phone buzzes again. I shoot her a look and dig my phone out. It's Judge. And this isn't the first time he's called. *Fuck.*

"I gotta take this." I disappear into the den, just off the main living room. Once inside, I accept the call. "Go for GP."

"'Bout fuckin' time you answer the goddamn phone, asshole."

I take in a deep, calming breath, allowing my eyelids to fall closed. "Sorry, Judge. I was in the middle of something."

"Yeah," he drawls. "I just bet you were."

I frown. I'm not sure what his angle is here. I wasn't late for a meeting. I wasn't expected to do anything for the club tonight. What the fuck is his problem?

"Rumor has it you've been nailing yourself a pretty little redhead," he says, a razor sharp edge to his tone. "The same fucking redhead I ordered you to leave the fuck alone."

Oh shit.

"Judge, listen—"

He cuts me off. "I won't listen to a fucking thing you say, asshole. Your chance to say your piece has come and fucking gone. You went against an outright order, putting this entire club on the line, all so you could play pants-off dance-off with the bitch who nearly got her ticket punched by some psychopath."

I sigh. "Judge—"

"Cut the shit, GP," he snaps. "You have thirty minutes to get here. And bring the redhead."

The call disconnects before I can say another word.

"Fuck," I snarl, kicking my foot out, knocking over a small stack of boxes beside me.

A soft knock lands on the other side of the open door, and I peer up to see Blair standing there, her eyes filled with worry.

"Everything okay?"

What the hell am I going to tell her? She knows I'm in the club, but she has no idea what that truly means. How will she react when I tell her she needs to come with me to the clubhouse? Or that it might not end well for either one of us, but it'll be worse if we don't go?

"I've fucked up," I tell her. "I haven't been totally up front with you."

"Okay," she says, drawing out the word with caution.

"You know I'm in a motorcycle club."

She smirks. "Yeah, I caught that part."

"Well, what you might not know is that my club... it's kinda like a family. A big, hairy, tattooed kind of family, but one I wouldn't change for the world."

"Um, okay. So how does all of that equate to you fucking up?"

I sigh. "I was told to leave you alone. The prez was

worried that helping you would bring too much attention to the club."

Her frown grows, and her cheeks flush with anger. "So you broke some kind of biker rule by helping me not die?"

"No," I say, attempting to keep my tone even. "But I did go against my club, and that shit just isn't done."

Seeming to come to some sort of decision, she throws her hands up in the air. "Fine. I'll leave, then," she clips out. She's already turned on her heel, moving back toward where we left her belongings. "Lucky for me, I haven't even unpacked yet."

"Blair," I admonish, moving along behind her.

"Jinx!" she calls up the stairs, refusing to meet my eyes. "Come on, kitty. We've gotta go."

Walter whines from inside the kitchen.

"Blair, stop."

Her eyes narrow, and her finger comes between us in a warning. "No," she snaps. "I never asked for this. I never asked to be attacked. I never asked you to come in and save me. I never asked you to creep around my house like a stalker. And I never asked you to go against whatever weird rules bikers live by. I just want to go home, have a shower, crawl into bed, and forget these past few weeks even happened."

"Red, stop." Stepping forward, I pull her into my arms. "Please, listen." Her shoulders shake with silent sobs. "I did what I've done for you because I wanted to. Because it was the right thing to do. Because you needed help, and I wanted to be the one to help you."

"But what about your club?" she asks my chest, not pulling out of our warm embrace.

"My club's pissed, but they don't know you, and they don't really know our situation. They're good men, Blair."

"I'll take your word for it," she grumbles.

I brace myself for her reaction. "You're gonna have to do more than that, Red."

She pulls away from my chest, peering up at me through narrowed eyes. "What does that mean?"

"It means, we're going there. Tonight. Now."

"And if I refuse?" she challenges.

"That'll piss them off more. And I would be very disappointed that you couldn't do that for me."

She contemplates exactly what I'm saying, her eyes never leaving mine. Seconds feel like hours while I wait, pretending to be patient, but feeling like I'm going to go insane if she doesn't say something soon.

Finally, she raises her nose in the air. "Fine. Let's get this over with, then."

I ignore the anger in her face and move in for a hug. "I'm sorry, Red. I never intended for any of this to go this way."

Her eyes flash with something I don't recognize, but

it's gone in an instant. She snatches a pair of jeans and a sweater out of her suitcase, then jerks the zipper closed with her lips pressed firmly together.

In one swift move, she lifts my T-shirt over her head, and then yanks the tie on the basketball shorts. My eyes follow as they drop to the ground, where they pool around her ankles. My gaze trails back up, and my dick twitches in my pants. Even pissed off, she's so fucking hot. She slowly dresses herself in her own clothes. *She knows it too.* She knows exactly what she's doing to me, and she's doing it on purpose. It's a punishment.

Tugging the sweatshirt on over her head, she pulls her hair up and out of the neck hole. After barking out, "Ready," she heads for the door.

I may not have known Blair for a long period of time, but one thing it doesn't take is a rocket scientist to figure out that when she's in this kind of a mood, it's best to just go along with it. That's why I don't say another word, and just follow her out to the garage. I stay silent as I climb on, firing it up. I wait patiently until she gets on behind me, and when her heat hits my back, I pull out onto the road.

The ride to the clubhouse is short, but for the first time ever, I almost wish it were longer. I have no idea what to expect. I crossed the line in a big way, and I was being honest with Blair when I told her that's just not done.

Like they're waiting for our arrival, two prospects open the ten-foot high chain-link gate as we approach, and then close it behind us. Several of the guys, and a couple of ladies, are standing around outside, beers clutched in their hands, and cigarettes dangling from their mouths.

I park in my usual space, and take Blair's trembling hand in mine.

"You're about to get yourself a new asshole," Twat Knot calls out.

I ignore him and the others who chuckle. It burns me to think these guys know my business, and have obviously been talking about it before we got here.

When I step inside, the music that's usually blaring through the speakers is missing, and everyone seems to be watching the door. We make our way into the main room. Footsteps sound behind us, and I glance back to see Twat Knot and the others following along, ready to take in the show.

In the center of it all is Judge, like a king on a throne —except, instead of jewels, he wears leather, and instead of a throne, he perches himself on a shiny chrome, Harley Davidson bar stool. His niece, Lindsey, sits to his left.

"Right on time," he notes, motioning for another beer.

"Lindsey?" Blair says, shocked.

Lindsey doesn't say anything, but she waves and gives me an apologetic smile.

I pull Blair up to stand beside me. "Judge, this is Blair Thompson. Blair, this is Judge."

Judge's eyes narrow on her before shifting back to me. "What part of 'stay away from the redhead' got lost in fucking translation, GP?"

"She needed me, Judge." It's the only answer I can give.

"And I need my fucking brothers to think with their heads and not their cocks!" he roars back, coming to his feet and leaning toward me. His eyes are filled with rage, and it's the first time I've ever seen that look directed at me. I drop my head, ashamed of how badly I let my club down. "You've been lying to me this whole damn time. And I'd have never known if it weren't for Lindsey seeing the two of you on campus. That's bullshit, GP. All for a piece of tail."

"First of all, my name is not '*the redhead*.'"

I whip my head up and around to gape at Blair.

Her shoulders are square, her nose in the air once again, and she looks pissed. "It's Blair, and I'd appreciate it if you used it."

I grab her by the elbow and give it a gentle squeeze, but she pays no attention.

"And second of all, I'm more than just an instrument for a man to use to get off with. I'm a woman, and GP has saved me on more than one occasion when the police wouldn't."

"I'd watch how you speak to our prez, woman," Karma says from behind us.

And that's when I break out of my trance of shame. "And I'd watch how you speak to Blair, Karma," I bark back. The room stays silent while he stares me down, but he doesn't say anything more.

"What are the Black Hoods known for?" I ask the room, but nobody answers. "Are we or are we not known for being vigilantes? The kind of men who'll go above the law and get shit done when it comes to helping someone in need?"

A reluctant rumble of agreement courses softly through the room.

I pierce Judge with a stare. "Prez. Normally, I don't go against a fucking thing you say, you know that. Your word is gospel to me, man. But this time, I had to do what any Black Hood worth the name would do. I stood up for the victim when the police dropped the ball. I saved the girl and kept her safe, and I'll keep doing that until we find the motherfucker who keeps harassing and scaring the shit out of her."

Judge steps forward. "You claimin' her, GP?"

I freeze. Is that what I'm doing? Is that what I want? Is that what she wants? *Fuck.*

"Yes, I am," I tell him. It's the only way. It's the only

way I can keep her safe and have my brothers support that. It's the only way Judge will allow this rescue mission to continue. And it's the only way I can keep these other slimy fuckers away from my girl. "Blair is mine."

Blair makes a choking sound beside me. "Excuse me? I'm not *yours*. I'm not *anyone's*, thank you very much. I'm a human being, not a possession."

"Blair," I warn, but Judge cuts me off.

"Woman, if you want our help, you'll shut your trap, learn our ways, and show some fucking respect in our clubhouse. GP claims you. That means you're under his protection, and also ours. Don't throw that gift in his face."

Blair's jaw tightens, but she doesn't say another word. I'm going to pay for this when we get home. And even though she's pissed, I can't help but smile at the idea of my house being our home.

BLAIR

THE ENTIRE RIDE back to the house, I clung to him, feeling the tension in his body. Once inside the house, he didn't say a word. He simply collected Walter from the bathroom and stalked past me to take him for a quick walk. This gave me plenty of time to stew on everything that was just laid before me with little warning.

GP is a far more dangerous man than I could ever have imagined. Even with the briefest of glimpses inside their stronghold, I knew just how dangerous they all were. The Black Hoods are the kind of men your parents tell you to cross the street whenever you see them coming, and I was just claimed by one of them.

He returns to the house, and Walter comes right to me. I try to focus all of my attention on him, and not the brewing storm that started earlier between GP and me.

"I know today was a lot to take in," he starts

cautiously. "A lot of that's on me. I should've told you more about the club."

"It was eye opening, to say the least. You claimed me in front of all your friends."

"I know, Red," he admits, rubbing his hands across his face. "It's hard to explain to someone who doesn't live the lifestyle. Hell, I didn't know if I wanted you to be a part of it until last night."

"Until you slept with me, you mean?"

"Yes. No. Fuck, I don't know. I like what's happening between us. I didn't expect Lindsey to rat me out, or that you even knew her. I wanted to take things slow when it came to the club. I knew if I tossed you in with them, you'd freak, but I wasn't given that choice."

Anger burns through my veins. "No shit," I fire back. "Between my attack, and now this, my brain has just had it. I don't know whether to be more scared of the guy who's trying to kill me or the people you call brothers."

"We're the good guys, Blair."

I arch an eyebrow. This group of men have likely killed other people. How could they be the good guys?

GP sighs. "Sometimes, we have to do bad shit to protect good people. I know it's hard to understand, but that's my life. That club gave me a purpose when walking the straight and narrow did jack shit." His eyes burn fierce, and full of truth.

He believes every word he says, and I respect that.

But I don't like how this was all forced on me. He had a choice, I didn't.

"I guess that explains why you took off the second the police showed up at the hospital."

"I don't give two shits about the police, Red. Had you not called me, you wouldn't be standing here. I would still be keeping you safe, but it would be from a distance. All I've wanted throughout this whole thing was to keep you safe and my club off the police's radar."

"But you lied to Judge about protecting me."

His frown deepens. "And I'd do it again. Don't you get that? No matter how hard I tried to stay away from you, I couldn't. You and me,"—he waves a finger between us—"we've been on a collision course from the second I busted into your house the first time."

He takes a step toward me. My head and my body fight against my heart. I want to take a step back from him. I want to scream at him for the extra drama he's brought into my life. But I don't.

He put everything important to himself on the line for me tonight. He lied to his president to protect me. He went against his family to keep me safe. Pulling away right now would drive a wedge between us that I don't think we could ever come back from.

"You don't have to be afraid of me, Blair," he says softly. "Have I done things that would scare you? Fuck yes, I have. But I don't regret them for a single second. I do terrible things to protect innocent people."

He's right, but my morality can't come to terms with the fact that he's claimed me as his property. "I just don't know what to think right now."

Reaching out for me, he pulls me against his chest, holding me as if he closed his eyes for a second, I would disappear like a ghost. "I fucked-up tonight," he mutters against my head. "But everything I did was to protect you. Claiming you made you safer."

"I know," I answer him, pulling away from his grasp enough to peer up into his dark eyes. "I just wish you would've told me all of this to begin with."

"I don't expect you to accept all of this tonight, but I hope you'll give me a second chance."

My heart and brain continue their war. My heart wants to forgive him without a second thought. My brain, on the other hand, says to run as far away from him, his club, and my attacker as I can get. To sell the house and start again somewhere else. But that's not me. I'm not that kind of girl. I don't back down from a fight. I don't run away.

My entire life has been one fight after another. My life is here in this town, at this school, and maybe even here with GP. I just have to take that leap and put my trust into the real GP standing in front of me now.

"You're right. I can't accept it," I start.

A flash of sadness courses through his eyes. I lift my hand to cradle his cheek, and he presses his face against it.

"But you've done more for me than anyone else in this world ever has. I can't just walk away from that. I'm willing to be open-minded if you can make me a promise."

"Anything, Red. You ask me to do anything, I'll do it."

"Don't lie to me. Ever. If there's anything else you need to tell me, I need to know now. No more blindsiding."

"The man you saw tonight, fighting for you? That's me. The real me. I'm the same guy I was, just with a different type of family watching my back."

I chuckle. *He is so right about his expanded family.*

"What?" he asks with a confused smirk.

"Most couples worry about their partner's family hating them. I just have to worry about which one of them is going to be following me around and scaring my classmates on campus."

"Couple, huh?" He smiles when he catches my slipup. "I like the way that sounds coming out of that pretty mouth of yours, Red."

"Well, I *am* your property now."

"Red, you're much more than property to me," he tells me sternly, before Walter pushes between us, forcing us to separate. "I see someone's trying to steal my woman away from me already."

I step back from GP and kneel in front of Walter. "He didn't mean that, Walter. You know you'll always have my heart."

Walter's heavy frame presses against me, almost knocking me to the ground.

"Traitor," GP grumbles under his breath, but Walter ignores him completely while I love on him.

Rolling over onto his belly, I scratch it, our lovefest continuing until a loud growl comes from the top of the stairs.

"Devil cat doesn't like you petting Walter," GP informs me.

I shrug. "She'll get over it as soon as I put her breakfast down for her in the morning." A yawn escapes me before I can stop it. "It's late, though. I think I'm going to head to bed. I've got class early tomorrow morning."

"What time? I'll make sure I'm up to take you."

"I'm pretty sure you're going to hear me get up if you're right next to me."

"I figured I'd be on the couch tonight," he admits.

"I'm not going to kick you out of your bed again." I grin up at him. "And wasn't it you who said I was safer with you? What's safer than you being right next to me?"

"Only if you're sure, Red."

I make sure I meet his eyes when I tell him, "I'm sure.

But you're going to have to be the one to tell Walter you're stealing his spot tonight."

"I saw you first," he huffs, walking over to the door and flipping the lock. "You two go on up. I'm going to check the doors and windows."

I grab my suitcase and head for the stairs with Walter in tow. Inside GP's bedroom, I spy Jinx lying right in the middle of the bed. The second she sees Walter, she jumps to her feet, hissing and arching her back in full-on attack mode. Walter steps back and hides behind me.

I take one step toward the bed and she runs off, making sure to take a swipe at Walter before escaping the room with her tail fluffed up. If things with GP and me work out, she's going to have to figure out a way to coexist with Walter.

But for the moment, I shake off the dilemma of how to make literal cats and dogs get along, open up my suitcase, and pull out one of my longer sleep shirts. Kicking off my shoes, I pull my shirt over my head and unfasten my bra, depositing them both on top of my suitcase. Slipping my sleep shirt over my head, my hands go for the button on my jeans, and a creak from the floor outside the door stops me cold. I spin, finding GP standing there, with a wicked grin on his lips.

"Don't stop on my account. I like the show."

"Hush, you." Unbuttoning my jeans, I shimmy them along my hips, down my legs, and let them drop to the floor. "Which side do you normally sleep on?" I ask him, straightening out my shirt.

"The side closer to the door." He pulls off his shirt, and I can't help but watch him strip down to just his boxers. He catches me. "Don't get any ideas, Red. These boxers are all mine."

"Good grief. You wear a guy's boxers once in a pinch, and it becomes this whole thing," I answer him, slipping into the bed.

Flipping off the lights, he joins me, his arms reaching out to grab me by the hips. Scooting his body closer, he cradles my ass against him. Walter hops on top of the bed, trying to wedge his way between us, but he gives up and moves back to the floor, whining.

"Poor Walter," I mutter.

"He'll be fine. But, if it makes you feel any better, we can get him a nice new dog bed tomorrow after your class."

"Deal." Silence lingers for a few moments between us.

"I like holding you, Red," he whispers, before his breathing begins to slow, and soft snores fall from his lips.

"I like it when you hold me too," I whisper back, before falling asleep in his arms, safe and sound for the first time in weeks.

GREENPEACE

"WHAT ARE you so fucking chipper about?" Twat Knot asks from behind me as we make our way down the unmarked trail. "Judge tears a strip off you and gives you one of the shittiest jobs he can, and you're still grinning. That redhead must have a golden pussy."

I'm typically pretty good at dodging Twat Knot's remarks. He's a funny guy... usually. But him even thinking about Blair's pussy is enough to make me want to bury him right here in this gopher infested field.

I spin on the spot, grab the front of his T-shirt in my fist, and tug him close enough to bite his fucking nose off if he says another word. "Her name is Blair, asshole. Not redhead. And she's my fucking woman now. It was made official, so if you say another word about her or her pussy, you'll be picking your teeth up with broken fucking fingers. We clear?"

Twat Knot's eyes widen. "Jeez, brother. Take a joke, would ya?"

Releasing him, I shove my finger into his chest. "This ain't the shit you joke about, asshole, and you know it."

He at least has the sense to look apologetic.

"And you must've pissed Judge off too, fuckface. Seems to me you're out here doing the shit job right along with me."

Twat Knot averts his gaze, mumbling something I can't understand.

"What?"

He sighs. "I said, I knocked a few motorcycles over the other night when I was drunk. Judge's has a big scratch on it now, and he's pissed."

For just a moment, I forget where we are. I forget we're standing in the middle of a field, skulking through the shadows, trying to find exactly where these guys are keeping all the dogs they plan on fighting. Instead, I picture the idiot in front of me knocking over a full line of bikes and Judge losing his shit.

Tossing my head back, I burst out laughing. Twat Knot's deep laughter joins my own, and the argument's forgotten, the way it should be with family.

Together, we wade through the dry grass until we come to the top of a hill. Down in the valley below, we see it. The old pig farm appears rundown and dilapidated. Every single window in the house is broken. Shingles are falling off or missing completely.

The barn, however, looks like it's been spiffed right up. It has new boards in random places. Men walk along the roof, hammering in fresh shingles. People wander in and out of it, carrying old furniture and hay bales. The sound of whining dogs reaches my ears, but as much as I want to go down there right now and rescue every single one of them, I know I can't.

I have to be smart. Judge needs me to be smart. He's already pissed at me as it is.

"Think they're keeping them in the house," Twat Knot surmises, handing me a pair of binoculars and points.

I follow his finger and peer through the lenses. Through the broken windows, I can see rusted cage bars, and movement here and there. It's too far to tell for sure, but I think Twat Knot's right. The barn is where the fights will be held, but that house is full of abused and starving dogs, just waiting to be sacrificed by a bunch of sick individuals with no appreciation for life.

As much as I hate the rift between Judge and I right now, I don't believe him sending me on this run was a punishment. I believe he sent me because he knows how much I want to end these fuckers. That I'll do whatever it takes to make sure the Anderson brothers never get a chance to regroup and start a new fight ring.

"'K," Twat Knot says. "I got a ton of pics. Let's get outta here before one of these douchebags sees us."

He doesn't need to tell me twice. I want to help these dogs, but there's not a damn thing I can do right now. Hence why I can't stop thinking about Blair. Ever since her little not-so-pleasant introduction to the Black Hoods, things have been a bit strained between us.

She pores over her schoolwork late into the night, and as soon as she gets up in the morning, she's in the shower, and handing me a coffee on our way out the door. She's beautiful and intelligent. She's far too good for me, and I worry I may be losing her already.

If I thought she was pissed about me claiming her, she was absolutely livid about the prospect on her tail. It's common practice in the Black Hoods for a prospect to tail, assist, or protect any member's old lady if the situation requires it. I tried to tell her that, but I was smart to keep the term "old lady" out of the equation. If she didn't like "mine," she'd hate "old lady."

We make it back to our motorcycles without incident, and Twat Knot shoots me a wave before starting up his and heading off down the highway. Guess that means I'm the one who has to update Judge.

"Yeah," he barks into the phone.

"Just finished scouting 'round the old pig farm," I tell him.

"And?"

"Oh, they're there all right. The barn has quite a few upgrades happening right now, and I'm ninety percent sure they're housing the dogs inside the old house."

"Did you see either one of the Andersons kicking around?"

"No. Looks like a whole new group of guys. I didn't recognize any of them."

Judge draws in a deep breath. "Appreciate the update."

"Hey, Judge?"

"Yeah?"

"We good?"

He's silent for a few moments, likely imagining all the creative designs he could make with my intestines. "Almost, GP. Almost. Keep your nose clean and take care of your girl. We'll get there. But if you ever fucking lie to me again, I will personally tear your beating heart from your asshole and shove it down your throat. Got me?"

I don't know whether to laugh or be terrified, so "Yes, sir," is all I say.

"Good. Now go home and rest up. We have a lot more work to do before the fight on Friday."

The reminder of the upcoming fight makes every-thing else seem just a little less important. There are so many fucking dogs in that house back there. Dogs just like Walter. Dogs who have never known a kind hand, a good meal, or a run in the park. Dogs who have been destined to fight for their life, over and over, until they lose.

These bastards are going down, and this time, they won't be coming back from it.

BLAIR

GP WAS true to his word in giving me time to process his club affiliation and his claiming me over the following few days, only because his president had him running all over God's green Earth on some kind of mission that he couldn't, or wouldn't, tell me about the entire weekend and last night.

Sleeping alone in his house felt so odd, even with the prospect from the club parked outside on guard duty. I couldn't even take Walter for a walk or leave the house. The prospect—whose name I wasn't even told—took care of all that to keep me inside. It was frustrating, to say the least. Feeling free and trapped all at the same time.

GP's world is so unlike anything I've ever been a part of before. I just don't know how or if I can fully fit into it. Becoming a psychologist has been my goal for so long, that adding in something else so late in the game throws me for a loop. A big, leather clad, dangerous loop that could cost me everything.

I really like GP—maybe even more than like—but I can't stop thinking about what our relationship means for my future goals. Will his club be okay with me working with the general public, or even the police? There are so many what-ifs, my brain can't stop trying to sabotage the way I feel when he walks into the room and smiles at me, like I'm the only girl in the world. The way I feel helping him cook our meals, or the way he holds me at night, cradling me in his cocoon of comfort and warmth. I just wish I knew what to do.

Trying to take my focus off the brewing storm inside my mind over my morals, I work on catching up on my schoolwork from GP's bed. Without any furniture downstairs but his kitchen table, I turned his bed into a makeshift desk. My books litter the entire space, save for where Walter's curled up on my feet, keeping one eye on the door, watching and listening for any noise downstairs.

"Ugh," I sigh, staring down at my term paper for Professor Brewer's class. For a summer course, he sure isn't taking it easy on us. The paper—which in a normal semester, would've been our final project for a large portion of our grade—is my first assignment. Twenty pages minimum, with at least fourteen scientific references. I guess the bonus of GP being gone a lot this weekend is that it's given me more time to work on my project.

I finish typing out the last paragraph of my conclusion, after pulling an all-nighter to make the deadline. It helps that Professor Brewer cancelled his morning classes, giving me the day off to recover. I briefly proofread my work before saving and uploading it to the virtual dropbox for the class.

"It's done," I exclaim to Walter.

He cracks open his good eye and looks at me.

"Sorry, buddy. I didn't mean to disturb your nap."

He moves from his spot on my legs and resettles against my hip with his head draping across my leg, attempting to shove my laptop off of it.

"Just one more thing left, and then we'll snuggle," I tell him with a rub of his ears.

"I don't know whether to be jealous or happy that my dog finally likes another human being more than he does me," GP teases from the doorway, startling me.

I smile back at him. "Maybe both?"

He comes into the room and sits on the edge of the bed, where it's not covered by books or Walter. "What are you working on, Red?"

"Just finished my term paper, thank God. I thought that thing would never get finished."

Brushing my hair off my shoulder, he places a kiss

against my neck, causing goose bumps to cascade all over my body. "How about starting something new?" he mutters against my skin.

"Quit distracting me. I have one more thing left to do."

He pulls away from me and smiles. "Anything I can help with?"

"Unless you know how to write a stellar application to help me get the internship of my dreams in less than an hour, I think this job might be a solo one."

He arches his brow, smiling deviously. "Can I watch?"

I jab my elbow into his ribs. "Not that kind of solo."

"Good," he declares. "That's my job."

Good grief. This man is going to drive me crazy. I've never been with someone as outwardly brazen as him. In my past relationship—all one of them—I was the more dominant one. With GP, it's a whole new ballgame.

"Tell me about this dream internship. Maybe it'll help get those… creative juices flowing."

"If you keep talking like that, you're going to distract me all the way past the submission deadline. I missed it once, and I can't do that again."

"Can't help it, Red. I love the way you feel wrapped around me, and it's been a long weekend of not seeing you enough. I'll go get the shower going, and if you get done in time, feel free to join me."

He shifts from the bed and whips his T-shirt over his head. I don't miss him flexing. When I ignore him, or try to, he walks out of the room.

Get the application done. Don't think about him in the shower waiting for you.

"Fuck, okay. Think, Blair," I mumble to myself, bringing up the half-finished application from a few weeks ago for Professor Coates.

I find the new application he emailed me in my inbox, and work on copy and pasting over what I had already done into the new form. The only thing that's left is the short essay on why I want to work with him. I sit and think for a few moments before taking a deep breath and typing. I don't write about my experiences of being abandoned by my family, or even my attack. I talk about my passion for the field, and the words just flow until I've written nearly five thousand words. Satisfied, I save it, then send it on to Professor Coates.

"You look sexy when you're concentrating like that." GP's standing in the doorway, still wet from his shower, with a towel slung low across his hips.

Before I can catch myself, my mouth falls agape.

"How about we get back to me distracting you?" He pulls the towel free from his body, letting it land in a pile at his feet. Sauntering over to me, he uses his finger to push my laptop closed.

"You were done with that, right?"

Like he cares.

Taking away my laptop, he then gathers the books from the bed and sets them on his dresser. Only one thing stands in his way from enacting the devious plan so clearly written across his face. Walter.

"Get down," he orders, but the dog digs in even farther. "You've really turned him against me."

"Come on, buddy," I say, nudging him. "Someone thinks you're cockblocking him."

"Damn right he is," he grumbles. "I've got plans for you today that involve not leaving this room for at least four or five hours, or until we've both had our fill."

"Seems ambitious. What if we get hungry?"

"The only thing I plan on eating is you, sweetheart."

Walter takes his dear sweet time stretching before finally jumping down onto the floor. GP moves to the edge of the bed, grabs my ankles, and pulls me toward him in one swift movement. I yelp in surprise, but silenced when he leans his muscled body over me, kissing me deeply.

My fingers claw at his hair, bringing him closer. If there's one thing I can't get enough of, it's GP's kisses. I've never felt more desired, more beautiful, or more worshipped than I do when he presses those perfect lips to mine.

Cupping my breast, his thumb strums my nipple, causing butterflies to go wild in my belly. I don't know how he's doing it, but I feel each swipe straight down to my core.

"God," I moan against his mouth.

Pulling away, he holds my stare as his hands yank at my shirt. It's up my arms, over my head, and in a heap on the floor faster than I can blink. My bra quickly joins it, and I flush a little when he drops to his knees in front of me.

Cupping both of my breasts, one in each hand, he laves at my nipple with his tongue. He nips, licks, sucks, and blows. And just when I think I could come from that alone, he switches to the other breast.

"Ohhh," I cry, tugging at his hair. Not hard enough to hurt, but enough to let him know I need more. I need him.

He presses a soft kiss to each tight bud and pulls away. "Slide these pants off, Red."

My stomach flops at the hunger in his eyes. God, he's so fucking hot, and it's me he's looking at like that, not some other girl. It's me he wants. It's me he's hungry for. Suddenly, I want to be his good girl, so I do exactly what I'm told.

I lift my bottom off the bed, hook my thumbs in my waistband, and slide my jeans down over my hips. Once they're over my thighs, he pushes my hands away, drags them down my legs, and tosses them over his shoulder.

Now he stands over me, where I sit on the edge of the

bed, leaned back on my elbows wearing nothing, because I still haven't bought any new panties.

"You are the sexiest fucking woman I've ever seen," he mutters, his voice thick with need.

I lie before him, and revel in the trail of his gaze burning its way across my skin.

"Spread your knees for me."

I inhale slowly through my nose and part my knees just a little.

"More," he says, his eyes pinned on my core.

I open them a little more.

"More," he growls, and this time, I almost don't recognize his voice.

Spreading them wider, his eyes devour me as he stands there, not moving. Just staring.

His knees hit the floor at the exact same time his tongue hits my clit. He takes it with one long, hard swipe. Then another, and another. "So fucking good," he says against my pussy. His breath hot, his tongue warm. Then, he slips his finger deep inside.

I gather the blanket beneath me in my fist as I watch him lick me. The sight is so fucking erotic, and I never want him to stop.

Finally, I can't watch anymore. I can feel it coming. My pleasure is taking over, and I'm about to tip over the edge.

I lie back on the bed and roll my hips. He sucks my

clit deep, flicking his tongue across it one way and then the other, faster and faster. His finger curls inside of me, rubbing along the spot all women crave to be touched, but few men seem to know about.

"Oh, God," I cry.

"Give me that, baby," he gasps, adding a second finger.

I feel his lips, his tongue, his teeth, his breath. I feel him. I feel me. I can't take another second.

I don't fall off the cliff. I fucking cannonball off of it, my body trembling. I make sounds I'm sure may be calling the Devil at this very moment, but I can't find it in me to care. All I care about is this man, and the mind-blowing fucking orgasm he's giving me.

"Holy fuck," I gasp as I finally come down.

"We're not done yet." Crawling up from between my legs, he pushes himself inside me.

Even though he's more endowed than most men, he fits inside me perfectly, like this is the way it was always meant to be. Like we were made for each other. Like I was made for him.

His fingers entwine with mine, and he raises my hands above my head. His lips meet mine in a slow, gentle kiss, and suddenly, the mood changes. He's no longer devouring me. He's making love to me.

As one, we move. Our hips rock in unison, our breath mingling between us. I feel every inch of him, and it makes me feel treasured. It makes him feel like a treasure to me. How did I get so lucky? How did I end up in this bed, being loved by this man? The adventure ends with me lying in the indescribable comfort of his arms with a smile on my face as we both drift off to sleep.

My stomach has other ideas, though. It lets out a growl, loud and long, waking us both.

"Come on, Red. Let's go feed the beast."

I pretend to be offended, swatting at him playfully as he leaves the bed. He disappears down the stairs, and I try to wake myself up while still reveling in the bliss of what we just shared. With all my doubts about his life and his club, it's the moments when we're together like this that gives me hope that we can figure out how to make this work. Curling up in his spot, I begin to fade off until Walter's cold nose presses against my hand, shocking me awake in an instant.

"I know, I know," I grumble. "I need to get up." It takes a minute, or three, but I finally force myself from the warmth of the bed and dress quickly in a pair of black lounge pants, and one of GP's oversized shirts.

My phone dings from somewhere nearby. I look for it, but it's not where I left it earlier on his nightstand. Walking to the landing outside of his room, I call down, "Did you move my phone?"

"It's charging in the bathroom," he calls back. "Unlike you, I know how to keep it charged."

"Very funny," I yell back. Pivoting, I head to the bathroom, and find it sitting on the bathroom counter, plugged into my wall charger. Entering my password, I go to the shortcut I made for my school email and scroll through them until one of them stops me. I quickly open it.

"Oh, my God!"

GP calls my name from downstairs, but I don't answer him. I'm too busy reading the words on the screen in my hand. His heavy footfalls running up the stairs alert me that he's coming up.

"What's wrong?" he gasps. His eyes are wide, his face pale.

I can only grin as I thrust my phone into his hands, watching as he reads. He looks up at me with an annoyed, but happy smirk.

"I'm a finalist for the internship!" I squeal, clapping my hands together in excitement.

"That's great, Red," he says, his tone dry and unimpressed. "But could you start with that next time? You damn near gave me a heart attack."

"Sorry," I mutter, rereading the email again. "It kind of just slipped out. This is the kind of opportunity I've been waiting for, and I did a bad job about containing it, given the particular situation right now."

"Tell me about it," he teases. "So, what's next with the internship?"

I scroll through the message, reading it aloud. "I have to setup an in-person interview for tomorrow with the professor." My voice falls as I continue to read it.

"That's good, right?"

"It is. But if I get this, it means my entire career trajectory could change. The last intern who worked for him was offered a job at his clinic in London."

"If that happens, we'll figure it out, Red."

God, what have I done to deserve this man?

Pulling me into a tight embrace, a loud crash, and a voice calling from downstairs interrupts us.

"GP? Dude, you okay?"

"Shit," he mutters. "I forgot about the prospect. He must've heard you yelling from outside." He steps to the edge of the stairs. "We're fine. Be down in a second." Returning to me, he reaches out for my hand. "I think it's time you meet your new shadow."

We head downstairs, hand in hand, and find a younger male with long blond hair, and a leather vest similar to GP's standing in the entryway, looking like he's ready for a fight.

"What the fuck was that all about?" he asks.

"Sorry," I say with a smirk. "I didn't mean to scare you. I'm Blair, by the way." I break away from GP's grasp and extend my hand to him.

The guy looks right past me to GP, who shakes his head no.

"He can't even shake my hand?"

"Prospect can't touch patched property without permission," GP offers.

I glare back at him. There's that word again —*property*. He knows how I feel about that.

"Seriously? It's just a handshake. It's not like I'm trying to seduce him."

He narrows his eyes at me.

"I like her, GP," the prospect says with a laugh. "She doesn't take shit."

"Shut up, Priest."

I step away from him, and this time, I take the guy's hand and shake it.

"It's nice to meet you. Thanks for watching me this weekend while he was gone."

The prospect releases my hand instantly, and backs away from GP, who's now pressing against me from behind.

"Not a problem, m–ma'am," he stutters. "I best be getting back to my post now that I know y'all are okay."

"Do that," GP snarls.

The prospect nods his head to me and leaves. The second he's outside the door, I spin around and stare at GP with my hands on my hips.

"You could've been nicer to the guy," I snap. "Why didn't you invite him to stay and eat with us?"

"You're pissed at me because I wouldn't let you shake

his hand or invite him to dinner? God, Red. You're too fucking cute," he laughs.

"You were rude to him," I say, not about to let this go.

"Sweetheart, this isn't a garden party. This is his interview to get patched into the club. He follows the rules, he gets a shot at the full vote. He's not going to step over the lines because you want to be polite."

"Still, you could've been nicer to him."

"What in the hell am I going to do with you?" He shakes his head while he continues to laugh. "Come on. Let's get you fed, and you can teach me all about manners."

Chapter 24

GREENPEACE

I CAN'T REMEMBER the last time I spent the morning just relaxing at home. It doesn't help that I don't have a lot of furniture, but today, I couldn't care less about the eight hundred unfinished projects waiting for my attention, or the lack of seating options in my home. All I care about is getting my woman another coffee, and cherishing the next few minutes with her before I have to take her to school.

Blair feeds Walter yet another piece of bacon off her plate, and I watch with amusement. She grins at him, patting his head while he devours his treat. Jinx sits in the doorway, watching, her tail curled around her front, the end flicking from side to side.

"Devil kitty's pissed at you," I tell her for the millionth time.

Glancing over at her cat, she rolls her eyes, just as her phone dings with an alert. "If you weren't so grouchy, you'd get more love too."

Blair reaches for her phone, taps on the screen a couple of times, and her face drains of all color. "Oh, God," she whispers.

"What's the matter, baby?"

Turning her phone to face me, she thrusts it in my direction. "I can't do this anymore, GP, I just can't. I can't take never knowing when he's going to invade my life in some way. As much as you say I'm safe from him, he still finds ways to get to me."

Plucking the phone from her hand, I look at the email.

"Your new boyfriend will die trying to save you," I read aloud. "Motherfucker!"

Rage boils over inside of me, and I push myself to my feet. First, he attacks her, nearly killing her. Then he stalks her, breaking into her home when she's in the shower. Then he leaves a creepy fucking note in her lingerie drawer, stealing all her goddamn panties, and now an email. And I still have no clue who this mother-fucker is. Nothing. He's a ghost. Untouchable.

I pace the floor, reading and rereading the email he sent. Not only is it a threat to her, it's a threat to me. And it's saying he's nowhere near ready to leave her alone.

"You don't recognize the email address?" I ask, handing her back the phone.

She stares down at it for a moment, thinking. "It's one from the university, but it doesn't have a name attached to it, which is weird. Usually our school emails include both our first and last names. This one's all random letters and numbers."

I stew on that for a minute. Is this dude someone from her school? Someone she knows? Maybe some psychopath who's seen her around campus and became obsessed?

"Get dressed," I tell her, coming to a decision.

"Why?"

I collect our plates from the table and take them to the sink. "We're going to the clubhouse. I want to show this to my buddy, Hashtag. I don't know shit about technology, but he's a computer whiz. If anyone can figure out who sent that, it's him."

Blair stands, looking uneasy. "Shouldn't we take this to the police first?"

I snort. "Fuck the police, Red. What have they done to help you? The only thing that detective is interested in is getting paid, and making it through to retirement without having to do any real fucking police work." I jab a finger toward her phone. "This is club business now. We take care of our own."

I have to give Blair credit. After the way she'd reacted

to being referred to as my possession, I assumed she'd clap back at my last statement. But she doesn't. Instead, she nods, stands up from the table, presses a kiss to my stubbled cheek, and disappears up the stairs, both Walter and Jinx in tow. Within minutes, she's back downstairs and ready to go.

"Grab your laptop, just in case he needs to look at that too."

She doesn't argue. Grabbing the laptop, she takes one final swig of her coffee, and follows me out to my motorcycle.

It's still early at the clubhouse, but Hashtag will be there. He's always up most of the night, and then awake and on the go early in the morning. I don't even think the man sleeps, to be honest.

Sure enough, when we step inside, he's standing in the kitchen area, pouring himself a steaming cup of coffee. He raises a brow when he sees us. "Morning, fucker," he greets me. "And Blair."

I grin. Looks like he remembers Blair's little rant about her name not being *redhead*. "Just the man we were looking for," I tell him. "You got time to look into something for me?"

"Sure, man. What's up?"

I motion for Blair to hand me her phone.

Taking a second to unlock it, she passes it over.

"Blair got an email from her stalker this morning. It's

a strange email, but I'm wondering if it might give us a clue. Maybe you can figure out who sent it?"

Hashtag takes the phone from me and examines the screen. I watch his face harden at the message displayed. "Oh, I'll figure it out. If I can't figure out who, I can at least figure out where. The location it was sent from may point us right to this asshole."

"I brought my laptop in case you need it too," Blair says, offering the slender computer to him.

Nodding, he takes it, then disappears out into the common room. Keys click, and noises chime as he types. I watch over his shoulder, but I know fuck all about this. Minutes pass, and then finally, he pushes back from the table he's sitting at. "Bingo, motherfucker."

"Did you find him?" Blair blurts, hope burning in her eyes.

"Not quite," Hashtag replies, an apology in his tone. "But I did figure out where. This email is one made through the university, which I'm sure you knew. What's odd about it is that even the background information is all anonymous. Whoever set it up has access to, or has hacked in to, the administration's system."

Blair's worried gaze meets mine.

"So I don't know who the email address belongs to, but I can tell you the email was sent from the campus. From the building at 745 Hyatt Road, to be exact."

Blair's eyes widen. "That's one of the psych buildings. The one where I have most of my classes."

Hashtag shrugs. "Sorry I can't tell you more, but it's obvious to me that whoever it is doing this shit to you is someone you see on campus."

Motherfucker.

BLAIR

WE SPENT a couple of hours arguing about my safety on campus when we got back to the house last night. GP was adamant that I not return to school until they had this guy out of the picture. As much as it terrifies me to go there, not knowing who this guy is, there's no way I'm going to let him change my life. I'm not going to hide or live in fear because of some asshole in need of a psychiatric evaluation. I refuse to put my dreams on hold for some pervert.

GP didn't like it, but he understood. It took some convincing before he finally conceded, but not without new restrictions. If I'm going to campus, he would be going with me, and not just to drop me off. Where I go, he goes. Maybe my professors and classmates won't notice him. Hell, who am I kidding? They'll definitely notice him, and his equally intimidating prospect who'll follow us to campus too.

GP parks his bike near the entrance to the main psychology building, where my interview with Professor Coates is being held. Every single head turns to gape at us when Priest's bike pulls in behind ours and parks.

"Do you really think I need both of you to protect me on campus? This isn't necessary." My cheeks burn as I peer over my shoulder, and lose count of the number of students and professors taking in my entourage. Just what I was afraid of—an audience.

"We can go back to the house if you'd like. You know how I feel about this." GP helps me off the bike before dismounting himself.

He hates it. With every fiber of his being, he hates that I'm not holed up back at the house, hiding away from the world. Am I in danger? Yes. But I can't keep hiding in the hopes that whoever this is forgets about me and moves on. If his email is any indication, my attacker isn't giving up. In fact, he's ramping up his attempts to keep me living in a perpetual state of fear.

"No. I'm not missing my interview with Professor Coates today."

"You mean more to me than a damn interview, Red." Frowning, he hands me my book bag from out of his saddlebag. "This guy knows about me. The only way that's possible is if he's seen us together."

"And in case you haven't noticed, I have two big, scary men watching my back. I'll be fine."

"I still don't like this. You're exposed here."

"I'm also surrounded by a large number of people. He came after me when he knew I was alone. He won't try anything out in the open like this." Or so I hope, anyway. Priest strolls up to the two of us, interrupting the rehash of last night's argument.

"Where do you want me, GP? Which building?"

"That one," I answer, pointing out the smaller of the campus psychology buildings to the left of us. "His office is on the second floor."

"If it's okay with you, I'll stick around out here and keep an eye out." A gaggle of women pass the three of us, their eyes locking onto both guys flanking me, and not moving.

"Eyes on the target, prospect," GP warns Priest when he catches him staring back. "This ain't the time to be scouting for pussy."

"I got you and your lady," he assures him. "Text me when you're done inside."

"Will do. Keep your eyes peeled for anything suspicious, and not on the ladies. If this slimy fucker's been watching Blair, this place is the most obvious. You see something out of the ordinary, send a picture to Hash."

Priest answers with a nod and moves toward a sitting

area in the center of the paved walkway, giving him a view of all the surrounding buildings.

"Let's get this over with," GP grumbles, reaching down to take my hand.

I lead him straight to the psychology administration building, trying to avoid eye contact with any of my peers. GP follows me closely up the stairs to the second floor. So close, in fact, he nearly bowls me over when I stop right outside of the professor's office door.

"Nice brake lights, Red," he says with a laugh. "This the place?"

"It is. And you're staying outside."

"The hell I am," he argues. "You agreed to my deal. You're not leaving my sight. I can't see you through a closed door."

"I'm going to be inside a room with no other exit. You'll be on the other side of the door."

"Not the point."

"GP...," I trail off.

"I said no," he growls back.

"Please," I beg him, batting my eyes like a child.

"That doesn't work on me, Red, no matter how cute you look."

"Please, let me do this alone. If you go stomping in there like a bull in a china shop, I won't have a snowball's chance in hell of getting this internship."

He stares at me, his jaw ticking as he thinks. Finally, his shoulders drop. "Fine," he mutters. "But if I hear so much as one sound I don't like, I'm coming in there whether you like it or not."

"Thank you. I know you didn't have to agree to this, but I appreciate that you're trying."

"You have no idea, Red. Now get in there, and get this thing in the bag. I have plans for you tonight."

After giving him a quick kiss on the lips, I knock on the door. A voice beckons me to step inside Professor Coates's office.

What lies on the other side of the door is a bit unexpected. Unlike the other professors in the program, his office is sparsely decorated. The two large, built-in bookshelves flanking his large wooden desk are bare. Not a single book in sight. I guess traveling around to different universities means you travel light, but I would've expected to see a family photo or something decorating the space. There's nothing at all.

Professor Coates peers up from over his open laptop. His large, dark eyes seem to bulge in the dim light of his office.

"Please, have a seat." Waving to the lone wooden chair in the room, he continues to type for several minutes, then finally snaps his laptop shut with a thud. "Sorry about that."

"It's okay," I assure him. "I hope I'm not too early."

"Not at all. I'm rather glad you could meet with me on such short notice. I was afraid you'd turn me down," he admits.

I can't hide my frown. Why would I turn down an offer to be interviewed? This is what I'd applied for.

Shoving away from his desk, he drags his chair around it, stopping at the corner, only a few inches away from me. "Ah, that's better. I can see you much better in this light."

I press my lips together at his closeness, but he just smiles back at me.

"Tell me about yourself, Blair."

"Oh, um… I guess there's really not much to tell that I didn't already say in my short essay response on the application."

"Your essay was superb," he assures me in his thick, British accent. "But it has no insight on you as a person. The passion you have for your studies are quite apparent, but I want to know you." Professor Coates reaches out and places his hand over mine.

My belly rolls with unease. "There's not much to tell. I've lived here my entire life—"

"Not possible with what I've heard about you, Miss Thompson," he concludes. "A woman such as yourself must have a fascinating personal history."

"My letters of reference and lists of academic accomplishments make me more than qualified for this internship."

Professor Coates's jaw clenches ever so slightly.

"If you'd tell me what exactly you'd like to know, I'd be better equipped to answer your question."

His gaze shifts to the floor, then back to me. "You're right. Your qualifications put you right on the top of the pile. However," he continues, crossing his legs, "I like to get to know my interns on a more... personal level. My research here is crucial to a new theory I'm developing. This position will need the special touch of someone who is just as passionate about it as I am." He pauses and presses his thin lips into a smirk. "Are you single, Miss Thompson?"

I frown. "I'm sorry, but how is that even relevant? I'm not sure you can ask me that."

"I apologize for offending you. Nothing can interfere with my work. Distractions cannot be afforded. I am merely inquiring if you have such distractions in your life."

The professor sits in his chair, watching and waiting for the response he won't be getting. My personal life is none of his business, especially with my "distraction" sitting right outside of his office.

I peer over my shoulder. GP obviously didn't hear him ask me that through the door. If he had, he'd have busted it down already. "Can you elaborate a bit more about the research?" I ask, trying to deflect away from his uncomfortable question.

"Yes, you're right. I should have started with that," he apologizes. "My research is that of a delicate nature, I have to admit." His gaze hardens upon me again, and he stops talking.

"Professor?" I ask, becoming more uncomfortable by the second.

He gives his head a gentle shake and clears his throat. "Yes, sorry. Where was I?" He touches his fingers to his lips. "Ah, yes, my research. I'm working on an extensive study on courtship violence. More specifically, the role of the perpetrator. There's been some interesting papers published in the last year equating histories of past violence in childhood to a predisposition to the continuation of violence in adulthood during courtship."

Shit. "I take it you've seen the papers and the news."

His face doesn't hide his knowledge at all. He knows about my attack. *Goddammit.*

"I didn't want to bring it up, but I am aware of your incident." He shifts in his chair abruptly, crossing his legs. "I understand that knowing now what my research entails, it may be uncomfortable for you to work with such subjects. But I believe whole-heartedly that your experience will enrich this research further."

It figures. That's why he's so interested in me. My

attack fits into his research. The subject and an intern wrapped into one convenient bow who wouldn't have to be paid for their time.

"I'm not sure how I could help, Professor Coates. I'm the victim in my scenario, not the assailant."

"That's precisely the reason why you'd be a great candidate for this program. Your insight on the mind of a surviving victim may prove helpful with the incarcerated individuals I've secured to interview." His dark eyes lock with mine while he theorizes the potential to exploit my attack.

"As in, convicted criminals?" The thought of stepping into a confined space with someone who's killed makes my stomach churn with discomfort.

"Yes," he answers flatly. "Violent offenders. The worst of the worst."

A flurry of hypotheses flicker through my mind. The person on the other side of that table could hurt me, or worse—be or know my attacker. A cold sweat breaks out all over my body. My hand falls to my stomach, praying that I can soothe myself and calm the storm churning inside of it.

"Are you okay, Miss Thompson? You seem flustered."

"I'm fine," I lie. I'm far from fine. *Don't throw up. Don't throw up. Don't throw up.*

"Are you sure?" He reaches out for me a second time.

This time, only lightly touching my hand. "Can I offer you something to drink?"

"Please don't touch me," I snap, jumping to my feet. His incessant need to make physical contact is disturbing. I've always been told he was a sworn professional, but his comments and touches are making me think otherwise. "Professor Coates, I have to be honest. I don't think this internship is right for me. I'm sorry for wasting your time." Without a second thought, I bolt for the door, but somehow, he's already there before I can reach for the handle.

"Please reconsider." His sharp tone throws me off. "You're the best candidate for this position. I don't want you to miss out on this opportunity."

"I'm sorry." Tears prick at my eyes. "But the answer is no."

"Red?" GP's voice calls from the other side of the door. "You okay?" The door handle jiggles. Then, the wooden door rattles in its frame as GP hammers his fists against it. "Blair, open the door."

Professor Coates steps aside. He doesn't say a word, and I open the door and shove past him, falling straight into GP's arms.

"The fuck is going on?" he growls, glaring over my shoulder. "Did he do something to you?"

"Please," I whisper, forcing back tears, "Let's just go home."

"Not until you tell me what's going on?"

"I didn't get the internship," I lie. If I tell him the truth—that the one man I admired only wanted to exploit my attack for his research project—GP would go ballistic. It's safer this way for us both. *I think.*

GREENPEACE

I'M STANDING in the hallway outside of Blair's classroom, waiting for her to finish up when my phone buzzes in my pocket. I don't recognize the number, but it's local.

"Hello," I answer, careful to keep my voice from echoing along the empty corridor.

"Is this the guy that goes by the name GreenPeace?" a man on the other end asks.

"Who wants to know?"

"Uh… it's, uh, Kenny. Kenny Dwyer." If this dude had declared himself Santa Clause, I wouldn't have been more surprised. Last time I saw Kenny, his face had been beaten to hell by yours truly, lying unconscious in a pool of his own blood.

"How the fuck did you get my number, Dwyer?" I

growl into the phone, my voice reverberating off the walls, echoing back to me. *Fuck.*

His words are rushed when he says, "It's not important. I need to tell you something."

I drop my hatred for the man long enough to hear what information he has to share. "Spit it out, asshole."

"The Andersons are on to you. They know the Black Hoods are watching them. They know you've found their new fight ring. They don't care, though. The Friday fight was a lie to trick your club. They're doing it tonight. Same time, same password, but tonight."

"Fucking hell," I mutter. "And how do I know you're telling the truth?"

"You broke my nose and my jaw. Do you know how much that hurts?" he whines.

"Not as much as you've hurt the dogs you helped train for fighting," I snap back.

Dwyer sighs. "I just didn't want you to think I lied to you. I don't want you guys coming for me again. And I don't ever want to lay eyes on that Stone Face dude again either."

I smirk. Stone Face does have that effect on people. "Appreciated," I tell him. "Now, if you're smart, you'll find an excuse to stay the fuck away from that pig farm tonight. What's about to happen isn't going to be pretty. Stone Face isn't the only scary motherfucker we have."

"Noted," Dwyer clips.

I disconnect the call and peer through the small window of glass in the top right corner of the door. Blair's back is to me, but even her back is hot as sin. I watch for a moment while she takes notes on her laptop, typing away, unaware I'm watching.

After a moment, I pull up Judge's contact info and call him.

"Yeah?" he answers, his attention not yet focused on our conversation.

"Just got a call from Dwyer," I inform him.

"Huh," he drawls. "Didn't realize you two were such good buddies now."

"Fuck you," I grumble. "He told me the Friday night fight was a lie. They're doing it tonight."

Silence follows my declaration. "Get your ass over here, and bring the prospect. I'm calling in the troops. This ends tonight."

I glance back at the doorway to Blair's class. "I can't leave her, Judge."

"You don't got a fuckin' choice, GP. You're needed here. She's safe. She's at school."

"Yeah, for another couple of hours," I growl. "What then?"

Judge curses. He understands my issue, but he's right. If we're going to break up this ring, we have to move, now.

"Let me call Lindsey," he says. "See if she'll stay with

her, drive her to the clubhouse at the end of the day. Then, when we're done, you can take her home with you."

"Lindsey's not exactly bodyguard material, man."

"Well, she's the best we got. Take it or leave it."

I slump back against the wall and stare up at the ceiling. "I'll take it. Call her."

"On it," he says. "Now, you and Priest get your asses here, *tout de fucking suite*."

He hangs up before I can comment on his shitty French translation. There's still another hour of this lecture for Blair. I can't call her right now, but at least she's safe in her classroom. I'll call her when it's over and bring her up to speed.

I head outside and find Priest at a picnic table. His eyes travel around the campus, taking in every single detail. I don't know what to think about this guy yet. I've heard good things, but he has yet to prove himself to me, and that makes me uneasy.

"We gotta go," I tell him, moving to where we parked our motorcycles.

"What about your girl?" he asks, jogging to catch up with me.

"Judge is sending his niece. He wants you and me at the clubhouse as soon as possible."

I'll give him credit. Priest does what he's told without much arguing. He moves out behind me, and we make our way through the campus and toward the clubhouse. I can feel the people staring at our bikes roaring along the busy, but quiet streets. A university is the least likely place to find a pair of tatted up bikers ripping up the roads.

We're the last ones to make it to the clubhouse. When we get inside, the meeting has already started. Priest steps outside because, as a prospect, he isn't privy to what goes on in our official meetings.

"Got ahold of Lindsey," Judge tells me, before I even have a chance to sit my ass in my usual seat. "She'll meet Blair outside of her class as soon as it's over. She'll stick with her throughout the day, and bring her here after they're both done on campus."

Although Lindsey isn't necessarily protection, I feel better knowing that Blair won't be alone.

"All right, assholes, listen up. Karma here has a plan, and I think it's our best shot of getting in and getting our hands on these sorry motherfuckers. It's the best way to keep any innocent people safe, and to keep any of us from getting pumped full of lead ourselves."

As Karma lays out the plan, complete with beer caps for us and peanuts for the enemy, I watch the clock. Karma's idea is genius. I just wish it didn't have to happen tonight.

After a bit more conversation, the guidelines are set out for tonight, and everyone spreads out, grabbing cold beers or making phone calls. The time changes on the clock. Red will be getting out of class right about now.

I step outside, call her, and wait through four rings before she finally answers.

"Hello?"

Hey, Red."

"Hey. You disappeared. I was worried."

"I had no choice, babe."

"I know. Lindsey told me. I don't know exactly what you've got going on GP, but please be safe while you do it."

"I'm always safe," I tell her. "You stay with your girl. She's going to bring you here to me at the end of the day."

"Okay," she says softly.

"And Red?"

"Yeah?"

I grin. "Charge your fucking phone."

Her laughter softens my worried heart. "I don't have my cord, smartass. And it's almost dead."

"Figures," I mutter. "I'll see you tonight, sweetheart."

"See you tonight," she returns. Neither one of us hangs up, but neither of us says anything else. There are three words that would fill in the silence, but we're not there yet. Are we?

"Goodbye, GP," she says, and hangs up the phone.

BLAIR

"I REALLY APPRECIATE YOU BABYSITTING ME."

After GP disappeared from campus today, I've been surprisingly thankful to Lindsey for stepping in as my chaperone. I never thought the idea of being on my own would scare me like this, but ever since I woke up this morning, an odd feeling has swirled around me like a growing storm. The tension in GP's voice earlier when he called isn't helping me shake it, either. His worry is only making mine worse.

"It's nothing." Lindsey smiles with a shrug. "I've been wanting for a little girl time with you, anyway. I'm really sorry about starting shit with GP and my uncle. I never would've said anything if I knew he wasn't clued in to y'all's relationship."

"That's between Judge and GP, not us. It's not like I

was in the know, either. I was just as blindsided by it as your uncle."

"I've seen him mad," she admits. "But never like that. Honesty is a big part of the MC life. GP broke that, but he had a good reason."

That night at the club house was, by far, the second scariest thing I've ever experienced—the attack obviously being first on that list.

"I know he did it for me, but there's so much I don't understand about the club life. Yet, here I am," I lament. "Property of a biker."

Lindsey abruptly stops, and turns to face me. "His claim means so much more than that, Blair. It makes you a part of the family. His family. My family."

"A family that scares the pants off of me."

"I thought that was GP's job," she teases.

"Is it that apparent?"

"Honey," she chuckles. "If you saw the way that man looks at you when you're not paying attention, you wouldn't doubt that at all."

"He makes me really happy," I admit, a foolish grin creeping across my face before I can stop it. "And it's not just because he's protecting me. It's so hard to explain. He literally crashed into my life to save me."

"The knight in leather armor riding a two-wheeled horse. How romantic," she swoons, with a little too much enthusiasm. "Oh, GP, you're so handsome," she mimics. "Damn right I am," she says, lowering her voice to sound more masculine. "Wanna bang?"

I toss my head back and laugh at her terrible impersonation of us. "Did you know we knew each other as kids?"

Lindsey's jaw drops. "See? That's exactly what I'm talking about. Hallmark level shit."

"So you don't want me to tell you the story, then?"

Lindsey grabs me by the arm, sidling up next to me. "Oh, I didn't say that. Spill."

"Don't you have a lab to monitor?"

Checking her watch, she smiles. "I don't have to be there for another fifteen minutes. And since you're not leaving my sight until I safely deliver you, as ordered, you can tell me all about the young GP."

We walk to the psych lab building while I give her the story. When I relay to her about how horrible he was to me as a child, she laughs so hard, a few students who pass by turn their heads to stare. We ignore them and trudge up the front stairs of the building, heading to the psych lab. The room is mostly empty, with the exception of a few students sitting at a back table, huddled together around a pile of books.

"How did you get conned into monitoring this lab again?"

"Extra credit assignment. It was either take the shift

in here, or write a huge term paper. Do you have anything to work on? Wedding plans, maybe?"

"Shut up," I giggle. "We've been together for like a week. A little early for that, don't you think?"

Rolling her eyes, she plops her bag down onto the table at the front of the room. "Hallmark card, Blair," she quips. "The way things are going, the two of you will be sucking face and saying those sweet 'I dos' in front of the club before the summer's over."

"You're crazy," I snort. "Not happening."

"If you say so." She pulls out a laptop from her bag and sets it up on the desk she's claimed. "You got any assignments to work on?"

I pull out my abnormal psych book. "About fifty pages of reading and notes to take."

"My shift is over at nine. If the place clears out before then, we can head out early. We wouldn't want GP putting out an APB if we're late."

With a laugh, I turn and deposit myself into an open desk not far from her. I open my book and try to get started, and she peers up at me a few times. But the longer I try to read the assignment, the more I think about what she said.

Is she right? *Shit*. This is crazy to be even thinking about so soon into the relationship. We haven't even said that we love each other yet, let alone gone on a date—unless you count dinner at his place. Why am I even thinking about this? I doubt he is. *Gah. Focus on your assignment. Read. Just read the words.*

I struggle for nearly two and half hours before the last student finally leaves the room. Lindsey bolts to the door to lock it. Another student walks up to the window, but she turns off the lights.

"Sorry," she calls through the window. "Lab's closed." The student tries to protest, but Lindsey just repeats herself over and over until they leave, smirking when she turns back to look at me. "What?"

I shake my head. "Nothing."

"Hey, I did my duty. I sat here. I monitored. They didn't say I had to stay the entire time."

"Right," I reply, packing up my book bag. Seeing my phone screen flash from inside, I pull it out, hoping to see a message from GP, but the only notification I have is a reminder to charge my phone.

"Get anything from lover boy?"

"No," I frown. Shoving my phone into my back pocket, I gather my bag and walk toward Lindsey, who's packing her own. "Is it normal for them to go so long without contact?"

"Once they bug out, there's no telling how long it'll be before they come home."

My frown deepens.

Dropping her bag on the desk, she walks over and pulls me into a hug. "I'm sorry. I shouldn't have said that." Releasing me, she assures, "They'll be fine. They're probably already celebrating their victory back at the clubhouse, which is why we need to get moving." Pivoting away, she snatches her bag from the table. "Ready?"

Nodding, I follow her from the room, and wait while she locks up behind us. The hot, humid summer air has turned cooler, and the moon shines down on us when we step outside of the building.

"Where's your car?"

"Not far. When Judge called me, I pulled it closer to campus. Follow me."

Lindsey makes a hard left around the corner of the building, heading toward the faculty parking lot. I stay close to her, my eyes scanning the shadows around us. She tries to make small talk, but the eerie feeling from this morning still pulsates through me. I try to ignore it, forcing myself to focus on Lindsey's chattiness.

A blue four-door sedan sits under the lone lamp in the empty parking lot. We start to pass a row of bushes near the edge of the lot, and one of them begins to shake.

"What the fuck?" I gasp, scrambling away. Lindsey jumps between me and the bush, pushing me back.

"Go to the car, Blair," she orders, tossing me her keys before pulling something out of her bag. "Get inside and lock the door. Call GP, now!"

I bolt from the spot and race to the car, my heart

hammering in my chest with every step.

"Come on out, fucker!" Lindsey yells, just as I make it to the car.

I fumble the keys with my shaking hands, sending them tumbling to the ground, where they slide under the passenger's side of the car with a jingle that seems to send shockwaves through the quiet parking lot.

"Fuck!" I sprawl onto my knees and sweep my hands everywhere for them.

"You've got to be kidding," Lindsey laughs. "It was just a cat."

I peer up from the pavement, expecting to see Lindsey holding a cat, but that's not what I find at all. Behind her, looming in the darkness, a tall figure with their face hidden inside a balaclava approaches.

"Behind you!" I scream.

Lindsey turns in slow motion, coming face-to-face with the man. She turns back to me, terror etched on her face. "Run!" she shrieks.

The sheen of a knife glitters in the moonlight. "No!"

My words do nothing to stop the figure's strikes on Lindsey, and she topples to the ground in a heap. The figure steps over her body and keeps striding forward, right toward me. Forgetting about the keys, I scramble to my feet, pulling out my phone to dial GP's number as I run around to the driver's side of the car. I glance up to find the figure getting closer.

The phone rings once, and then dies in my hand. Shit! I toss the useless heap to the ground and jerk on the car's door handle. It doesn't budge.

What the fuck do I do? Lindsey's hurt. My phone's dead. GP is God knows where. I'm alone, and the man I'm pretty sure has been stalking me is coming around the front of the car.

I scramble backward, but my feet stumble underneath me when I try to run. I only manage to take two steps before he grabs me from behind. Shoving his hand over my mouth, he uses the other to wrap around my chest, squeezing me so hard, I can hardly draw in a breath. I try to scream, but the sound is muffled behind his gloved hand.

"I told you you're mine, Blair," he whispers, his voice calm and smooth.

Fingers dig into my scalp and yank me back hard to the ground. I fight back, scratching and clawing my way to my feet, trying like hell to get away. I land a hard elbow to the attacker's stomach, forcing him back, but he retaliates. For a second time, he fists my hair, using it to slam my head against the side of the car. Once. Twice. Three times, until the world and my head begin to spin.

Only one thought lingers as the darkness takes me under.

I never told GP that I loved him, and now it's too late.

GREENPEACE

THE PLAN IS SIMPLE. Priest and one of the other prospects would attend the fight, like they're any other bloodthirsty patron. No cuts. No club affiliated clothing. They use the password to get through the crude security blocks and make their way to the front of the rings.

Once inside, they text Judge with an idea of how many armed men are posted around the building, both inside and out. The rest of us go in the back way, just like Twat Knot and I did the other day. Only this time, it's dark as hell, and we won't know if the Andersons have that part covered.

We raid them early, before the first fight even starts. We take out the staff, scare the fuck out of the patrons, rescue as many dogs as possible, and torch the place so they can't try this shit again.

"What the fuck's taking so long?" Karma grumbles, staring off into the night.

"Give them time," Judge says, exhibiting a patience I've never seen from him before. "That new guy might be an idiot, but Priest is a good shit. He won't fuck this up."

The words barely leave his mouth when his phone lights up in his hand. We all watch Judge check the text and wait for our instructions.

"There's two men posted at each door. Two men inside the house where they house the dogs, and two more running the dogs to and from the ring. Ten men in total, plus the Andersons, but they haven't been seen yet. All of them are armed, and will shoot you if they catch you."

I stare over his shoulder at the cars lining the long driveway, their headlights shining in the darkness like a billboard advertising the dog fights they're about to attend.

"We better move quick," Karma says, his eyes taking in the growing crowd. "The more people there, the more people we have to end."

This isn't the first time we've raided a fight ring, but it is the first time we've gone in with the intent to kill. In the past, we would break it up, bust some heads, and leave with a warning not to do it again. That tactic hadn't worked on the Anderson brothers, so it was time to try something new.

When Karma gives the signal, all eight of us charge over the hill, keeping low to the ground, counting on the cover of darkness to keep us from being seen. The others approach the barn, and Stone Face and I head for the house. If Priest's intel is right, there are only two men in here, and two who move between both buildings.

The first man goes down without us even firing a shot. One punch from Stone Face and he's out cold before he even knows we're there.

We move swiftly, stepping inside the house. Rusted wire cages line the walls, each one containing a dog. Most of them are pit bulls, or bulldogs like Walter. Some are snarling and barking at us, while others are lying on the floor of their cages, already given up.

Stone Face points to the stairs, and then to himself. I nod.

I watch him disappear up the old creaky steps, and then continue my tour of the main floor, careful not to get too close to the cages. These dogs might be innocent, but they're far from trustworthy.

A voice cries out from upstairs, followed by a loud thump, and then another. I stare up at the ceiling. *Please let that cry be from one of Andersons' men and not Stone Face.*

I turn into the kitchen, and come face-to-face with Kenny Dwyer. He gasps and raises his hands in the air, his plate shattering on the floor between us.

"What the fuck, man?" I hiss. "I thought you were going to steer clear of here tonight?"

Dwyer gulps. "I was, but after getting my ass kicked the other day, the Andersons were worried I said more than I should have. If I didn't show tonight, they would've known you knew."

I glare at him for a moment. It's an odd feeling when you loathe somebody and everything they stand for. But at the same time, you see they're trying to do the right thing, no matter how short-term that turns out to be for. Glancing around, I come to a decision. Pointing to a chair in the kitchen, I say, "Sit."

Dwyer looks at it, then back at me. If I didn't know any better, I'd think the man was about to piss his fucking pants. He doesn't argue, though. Like a good little bitch, he moves to the table and takes a seat in the old metal chair.

Grabbing a leash that's been left on the counter, I make a half-assed attempt at tying him up. "This is just for show," I tell him. "You stay here, and you don't fucking move. If one of my guys comes along, you tell them to talk to me before they deal with you."

Dwyer nods, his eyes wide with fear. "Thank you," he says, fighting back tears.

"Don't fucking thank me yet, asshole. I'm just delaying the decision on what to do with you."

I turn on my heel and make my way back to the stairs.

"All clear," Stone Face says as he reaches the bottom. Took out one up top."

I nod toward the kitchen. "Got Dwyer in there. Long fucking story."

Gunshots and screams float from the barn, and we both move toward the door to see what we can do to help. We reach the front porch, and Judge exits the barn, an identical man in each hand, the backs of their shirts grasped tightly in his hands.

"Gather 'round, boys!" he screams, and one by one, each of the Black Hoods steps out of where they were and into the light provided outside the barn. Patrons of the fight stand around us, all of them looking uncomfortable and confused.

"I know you sons of bitches came here to watch a fight to the death, but tonight, you get a special surprise. Ya see, those dogs in there, they're done fucking fighting for your entertainment. They've done their jobs in making these men rich."

Judge shoves the men to the ground, where they lie there, staring up at him in fear. "You people want to see a fight?" he hollers loud enough for everyone to hear.

"Yeah!" the crowd yells.

He chuckles. "I bet you do, ya bunch of sick fucks. And

you're in luck, 'cause we have a mad dog of our own, and he's going to take these guys on—two on one, no weapons. Fight ends when one's still standing. Ya with me?"

The crowd roars with approval, and I frown at Stone Face. He's the mad dog Judge mentioned, but this wasn't part of the plan. Stone Face grins, hands me his gun, and walks into the center of the circle, cracking his knuckles and rolling his shoulders.

"Someone get in there and ring that bell!" Judge roars. "It's time to start the fight!"

The fight is brutal and bloody. Even I can't watch.

This club has done a lot of things in order to save someone, or teach a bad person a lesson, but the gore and pain inflicted in this punishment is almost too much for me.

"This is just," Judge says softly, sidling up beside me. "This is what these men have done to these dogs for years. This is what they deserve."

"I know," I tell him. "I just can't stand to watch the evil of the people cheering it on."

"The world is filled with evil people," Judge laments. "The most dangerous ones are those who think that evil deeds are the natural choice. The ones who don't even know they're evil."

Flesh against flesh, and bone crunching bone. The sounds assault my ears, and I step inside the house to assess the dogs in the front hall. So many wounded. So many ruined. So many who will have to be euthanized.

"What's the plan for the survivors?

Judge's eyes soften when one bull dog limps from his pen and collapses on the ground at our feet. I kneel down, trying to comfort the poor creature as he labors to breathe.

"I called the rescue that helped us out the last time. Should be here soon to take the ones they can save."

All of a sudden, a loud roar rises from the crowd, and we both run outside just in time to see Stone Face use one man's head to crush the others. Three rams, that's all it takes. Three slams of head on head and they're gone. Their evil deeds are over, and won't affect anymore animals.

Justice has been served.

BLAIR

BRIGHT LIGHTS STIR me from the darkness encompassing my throbbing head. My eyes flutter twice, but the light burns. The marching band parading through my head relentlessly pounds away, making me want to go back into the darkness to escape it.

It takes a herculean effort to lift up my head to take in my new surroundings. The space is dimly lit and damp. The air in the chilly room clings to my damp skin. *Where am I?*

I will my body to move, but it just won't. Forcing my eyes open further, I find out why. My feet, thighs, and hands are bound to an ancient wooden chair. Any semblance of time has been torn away from me. The attack had occurred around nine, but without windows in view, I have no idea how to gauge how long I've been here.

"You're awake," a voice to my left says from the darkness. "I'm glad."

"Who… Who are you?" I croak.

The figure steps out from the shadows. The black balaclava still hides his face, but not his dark eyes. I'd recognize them anywhere. The same pair of eyes that had stared back at me from the other side of my door. The ones that had peered into mine as he held me to the ground. It's *him*.

He moves closer to me, like a predator sizing up its prey. "I was afraid I'd killed you."

Yeah…like he cared.

The way I feel, I honestly wish he had. This is only going to end one way—my death, and his satisfaction. Tears burn trails down my cheeks. All hope is gone. My call to GP never went through, and as Lindsey said, they could be gone for days. Precious days that I don't have. I'm on my own.

"Help!" I cry, trying to scream, but it comes out more of a whimper.

"No one's going to hear you down here. I made sure of that. Not even your boyfriend can save you now, or that ugly mutt of his."

He paces the floor in front of me, twirling a large knife in his hand—first one way, and then the other. Blood drips along its sharp edge as he moves. Lindsey's blood. *Oh, God, Lindsey!* My heart aches knowing her death stains my hands. He killed her for protecting me.

How could I have let this happen? She shouldn't have even been there. I should've told her to run. It should've been me dead on that sidewalk, not her. She didn't deserve that fate, but he's intentionally showing me the fruits of his murderous labor to taunt me.

"I'm sorry about your friend," he says, the happiness undeniable in his voice. "She would've made a fine addition to my collection." He looks away to an empty wall, like there's something there only he can see, but he jerks his gaze back at me with one swift movement. "She tried to stop me from taking you. You're mine, though. Mine!" he screams out that last word, his hands splayed wide in front of him, but he doesn't drop the knife. "No one takes what's mine."

I crane my neck to peer around the room again. *Please, God. There has to be a way out of here. Some way to escape lying right in front of me.* But, no. Nothing. There's absolutely nothing. Just my attacker and me, alone together in this pit of Hell, with my life hanging in his psychotic hands.

"It's your fault, you know," he continues. "You challenged me. You teased me with what I couldn't have, hiding away in that big house of yours with the cops always around." His voice cracks, and there's something familiar about it. It sounds off, like he's trying to change it somehow. "But I'm patient, Blair. I waited until even that boyfriend of yours couldn't protect you."

His pacing intensifies. Back and forth across the floor, his eyes never stray from me. They're like heat-seeking missiles locked on their target.

"You denied me three times before, but now, you can't run away from me. From us."

He stares at me for a moment, and in a flash, he charges forward. I try to shrink away, turning my head to protect my face from the impending impact, but he stops just short of it, teasing me, reveling in my fear. His hands move to the arms of my chair, and he brings himself down to eye level.

As much I want to believe it's not true, I know this man. I know I do. I've seen those eyes before. So why can't I identify him?

He leans forward, presses his nose into my hair, and breathes deep. He exhales, and his hot breath cascades over my skin. That sensation, mixed with his closeness, makes my stomach churn.

His head falls back as he moans in ecstasy. "I can smell your fear, Blair. Do you know what that does to me? What it makes me want to do to you?" He sucks in another deep breath, and his body trembles, my fear turning his excitement into arousal.

He shoves away from me, causing the chair to scrape across the floor. It wobbles, the movement straining the already vulnerable condition of its old wooden legs. Using my body weight, I shift to the best of my ability to keep it upright.

"Everything was perfect until your boyfriend got involved," he seethes. "The thought of him touching you revolts me. He contaminated you, but I can fix that. I'll purge his touch from you. Then," he growls, "then I can have you. All of you."

My eyes follow him, and he turns his back on me, moving toward a table in the far corner of the room. Humming to himself, he unravels a black cloth in front of him. Each movement reveals various tools inside the roll, each one in their own slots. He's not just going to kill me. He's going to torture me.

A renewed sense of self-preservation begins to stir inside of me. Maybe it's a last-ditch effort of my mind to prove to myself that I did every possible thing I could to save myself. A pointless one, as things stand now, but I have to try. Even if it only delays the inevitable.

Make him talk. Put the focus back on him. Professor McCallen's voice floats through my mind, a memory of one of my first lectures with her. *Someone who's verbalizing isn't hitting you.* I bite back hard, and try the only thing I have left.

"I shouldn't have done that," I apologize, keeping my tone flat and even to hide the lie.

He turns from his tools, his eyes pinning me in place.

I want to turn away from his gaze, but eye contact is key to making him believe I'm telling the truth. "I didn't realize just how special you were that day."

He doesn't move at all.

"It's my fault, all of it. I led you on. You attacked me because I provoked you." Every single thing leaving my mouth sends bile rising from my stomach and into my throat. "I'm sorry."

"Don't lie to me!" he shouts. "You're not sorry. You don't appreciate what I'm doing. You're saying that because you want to leave me, just like she did. Like they all did. But not this time. I'll make sure of it."

Think, Blair. Think. Fucking lie. Fight for your life.

He turns his back to me again, fingering a spot in his tools before selecting something long and silver. "Do you know what I like about knives, Blair?"

I watch in horror as he rubs his finger along the edge of the blade, hissing when it pricks his skin. He pivots, and cocks his head to the side. "Guns are too impersonal, too quick. But a knife,"—he waves it in front of him like a prize—"is a gentleman's weapon. A weapon meant to inflict harm, to take life slowly. It's perfect."

His walk is slow, but deliberate. His eyes narrow in concentration. Each step brings him closer and closer. I drop my eyes to the knife, feeling all hope drain from me. It's over.

"Let's see if your blood tastes as sweet as I remember." The knife plunges deep into my flesh, ripping a guttural scream from my lips.

"Please," I gasp. "I don't want to die."

"You were always going to die, Blair. Just like the ones who came before you. Just like my late wife. Everyone has to die."

GREENPEACE

PANIC HAS my heart hammering in my chest. It's funny how one minute we can be the conquering heroes, returning to the clubhouse, ready to celebrate a job well done in a world without the Anderson brothers, and the next minute, our whole world tips over the edge.

"Try again," I snarl, peering over Hashtag's shoulder at the screen on his computer.

Hashtag sighs. "I'm telling you, man, it's not showing up. If her phone's dead, it's not sending off a locator signal. End of story."

"Fuck!" I shove away from him and slam my fist into the wall. My hand disappears inside it, in a cloud of drywall dust.

Something's wrong, I fucking know it is. They should've been here by now. And neither Lindsey nor Blair are answering their phones. Judge sent the guys out, and they searched everywhere. My house. Blair's house. Lindsey's house. The school. The library. Even fucking Walmart. They weren't at any of them.

"Take a breath, GP," Judge says from behind me.

I don't know how he can be so fucking calm. His niece is missing too.

"Hash, try Lindsey's phone. Hopefully, wherever they are, they're together."

Hashtag taps away at the keys. It takes only a few moments before he glances back at us and grins. "Bingo."

I run forward and stare at the screen, like I have a clue what it even says. "Where?"

"Seventeen hundred Merwin Road." He types a few more things, and then his shoulders drop. "Shit, guys. That's the hospital."

"Fuck," Judge mutters, but I don't say a word.

I can't. I stand motionless, staring at the screen.

At the hospital. They could be hurt. They could be dead.

"Let's go," Judge says, clapping me on the shoulder as he passes.

I follow him out to the parking lot. It's just the two of us, as we're the ones with something to lose. Judge leads the way to the hospital, and thank God we don't pass any cops, because at the speed he set, we'd have our licenses taken on the spot.

Once inside, I follow him to the information desk. The lady behind it takes one look at him, then me, examining our tattoos and leather cuts. Her face pales. "May I help you?"

"Lindsey Sheridan? She may have been brought into emergency?" Judge asks.

Putting the name into the system, she reads something on the screen. "Are you family, sir?"

"I'm her uncle," he tells her. "I raised that girl as my own."

She gives him a sad smile. "She did come in by ambulance. She's in ICU."

My heart sinks. "And Blair Thompson? Was Blair Thompson with her?"

She types that name in as well, and shakes her head. "I'm sorry, sir. There's no Blair Thompson listed in our system."

I close my eyes and take a deep, cleansing breath. I don't even know how I feel about that news. On one hand, I'm glad she's not here, because that means she's not been found injured. On the other hand, her not being here means she's still out there missing. And if Lindsey's in ICU, something terrible has happened. *So where the hell is my woman?*

The lady gives Judge directions, and I follow him, my mind spinning, attempting to come up with something—anything—to help find Blair.

"Relax, bud," Judge says, his voice low. "We'll find her."

I don't argue. It's easy for him to say, though. He found his niece, and my girl's still out there.

Lindsey looks so small in that giant hospital bed. Tubes and wires are hooked up to her face and arms, machines beeping and whirring all around her.

"Excuse me," a nurse calls, hurrying over to intercept us. "Immediate family only."

"We are immediate family," Judge growls, pinning her with a glare, telling her she'd be fucking crazy to argue with him right now. "What happened?"

"The police were already here. We weren't sure who her next of kin was."

"I am," he states as he steps forward, taking Lindsey's pale hand in his dark, tanned one.

The nurse moves to the far side of the bed and fiddles with some of the equipment around Lindsey. "She's a tough girl," she tells us. "She came in here in an ambulance. She had a stab wound right through her belly, and some trauma to the back of her skull. She's lost a lot of blood. The doctors had to fix some internal damage from her stab wound, and we don't know yet what kind of damage she'll have from the head injury."

"What do you mean, you don't know?"

"She hasn't woken up yet. She's been given a signifi-cant amount of pain medication, but her unconsciousness is a result of the attack, not her medical intervention."

"Was there anyone around where they found her? Another girl?"

The nurse shakes her head. "I'm sorry. I don't know a lot, so those would be better questions to ask the police. All I know is that she was found this way by a student at the university."

That snaps me out of the hopelessness I'd slowly been sinking into. "Was she found on campus?"

The nurse nods. "In a parking lot, I believe."

I flick my eyes to Judge, and he nods. "Go."

Hope blooms in my heart and I turn, bolting out of the room. The prospects had said they'd checked out the campus, and all around the psychology buildings, finding nothing. But I have nothing else to go on. And putting one hundred percent trust in the word of a prospect is the last thing I'm about to do.

With the exit in sight, I punch in Karma's number and wait for him to answer.

"Yeah, man," he answers.

"Lindsey's in rough shape. She was found by a student. On campus." Karma curses under his breath. "I'm headed there now. Whoever did this knows the campus, and there's no way they'd have taken Blair far, not without being seen."

"On my way, with reinforcements."

I end the call and shove the phone back into my pocket. The entire ride to the campus, my head spins with different scenarios. Maybe this is some kid who goes to school with Blair. Maybe he drugged her and took her back to his dorm. What if it's a gardener or a fellow classmate? Someone who wouldn't be suspicious lurking around campus?

In the few times I've been to the school with Blair, her classes have all seemed to be located in one area. There's a park-like setting in the center, and a giant parking lot at the back of the block. From what I can tell, the psychology department's made up of about ten older, but well-maintained buildings.

Pulling into the parking lot, my blood runs cold. There, under a streetlight, surrounded by nothing but empty parking spaces, sits Lindsey's car.

The prospects had said there was no sign of the girls here, and for that, I'll have their fucking heads.

I park behind her car, and as soon as my engine shuts off, the roar of several other motorcycles rumble up toward me. It's Karma, and he's brought the others. One by one, they file into the lot and park alongside me.

Karma's eyes are pinned on Lindsey's car when he calls out, "Priest!"

"Yeah?" Priest responds, making his way forward through the small crowd.

"Why the fuck were we told there was no sign of the

girls on campus when Lindsey's fucking car is right fucking here?" He screams those last few words, his face filled with rage.

"I didn't check here, Karma," Priest admits. "I was sent to GP's and Blair's houses. Campus was on Burnt and the new guy."

Karma shakes his head. "I'll deal with them later. And you're sure the houses were empty?"

Priest nods. "One hundred percent. I almost got eaten by Walter when I checked out GP's."

"She has to be here somewhere," Hashtag growls, looking around us. "I did a quick check of the traffic cams around the area, and even though I didn't see Blair in any of them, I also never saw anything suspicious."

I glance at all the dark buildings surrounding us. "She's here somewhere. I can feel it."

"Let's split up," Karma announces, speaking louder so everyone can hear. "Move in pairs. We go building to building. We'll start in the basement and work our way up." He continues barking out orders, but I'm already on my way to the nearest building, Hashtag hot on my tail.

"We'll find her, man," he insists, coming up beside me.

"I won't stop until we do."

The building is locked, but I've never let a lock stop me before. A credit card and a hairpin are things I don't leave home without, and it takes just seconds to pop the lock and make our way inside.

This is the same building Blair and I were in earlier today. The same one I left her in when I got the call from Dwyer.

Room by room, we search. The basement is full of old boxes of papers, broken bookshelves, and old chairs. The upper floors have nothing but offices and classrooms. And no Blair.

We move toward the next building, and I hear the others moving about, calling out to each other, declaring buildings clear. *Hold on, baby. I'm coming.*

BLAIR

TIME MOVES EVEN SLOWER when I come around the second time.

For what felt like hours, I slipped in and out of awareness. Knives stabbed and sliced at my skin, even piercing in deep on more than one occasion. He was torturing me, reveling in my pain, in my fear.

Numbness eventually took over, and when it did, I didn't cry. I didn't scream. I didn't give him the satisfaction. He backhanded me then, angry that I wasn't playing into his game. That blow sent me into blissful unconsciousness.

I dreamt of GP and our life. I imagined what could have been if none of this had happened. How I felt in his arms when he held me. The way he pretended to hate Jinx, but deep down, really loved her. Happiness filled me, and love swelled in my heart. I fought to stay in that dream state, ignoring the ring of darkness along the edges that stained the one beautiful thought I had left.

I continue to cling to that thought as my attacker forces me back to the waking nightmare I'm living in with him.

"Good girl," he purrs, giving me another slap across my cheek. "I knew you wouldn't disappoint me. You're a fighter. You'll make me work to own you."

Every part of me aches. Blood pools from my stomach and thighs, dripping down onto the floor below me in repeating splats, seeping into the porous nooks of the concrete, leaving behind a trace of my fate. A piece of me that has already found its final resting place, while my soul will likely never find peace.

"Just let me go," I plead, tears streaming down my face as I struggle to breathe through the pain. "I won't tell anyone."

"We've been through this, Blair," he reminds me. "You're not leaving here. Not breathing, anyway."

He returns to the table where his last tools came from. This time, he doesn't pick something from inside the roll of knives, but comes back with empty, bloody hands.

"Tell me about the others," I implore him, in an attempt to distract him again. "How many were there?"

"I know what you're doing, Blair," he says, making his way behind me, brushing his hand against my cheek. He's only out of sight for a second before his fingers thread into my hair and jerk my head, slamming it against the back of the chair. "I've been doing this longer than you've been alive, child. You can't use my own tricks against me, the one who developed them."

And that's when the pieces fall into place. I know who it is behind that mask. The sensation of his fingers against my flesh burns like wildfire meeting gasoline. My body recoils, but he just digs them in harder. There's truly no escape from him.

"Watching all the hope drain from your eyes was almost as pleasurable as it was the night we first met." His hands wrap around my throat, his fingers digging into my flesh, cutting off my oxygen. My body jerks as I struggle to breathe. I try to squirm free, but he only applies more pressure.

"You look so much like my wife when I hold you like this, with the same terror in your eyes. She fought back too, you know, just like you. She tried to leave, but I stopped her." He inhales a shuddered breath. "No one leaves me, Blair. No one"

"Professor, please," I beg.

His eyes grow wild at my acknowledgement. Releasing my throat, he circles around to the front of me, his hands reaching to the balaclava still covering his face. His fingers trace the edges before he rips it over his head, confirming my worst fear.

My attacker wasn't some random person who found

me. The attack. The not so random encounters. The interview. He planned all of it from the very beginning. I'd been an unknowing participant every step of the way.

"For a smart girl, it took you incredibly too long to piece the puzzle together," he says, shaking his head with true disappointment. "I thought you were smarter than that. We could have worked beautifully together, Blair." Professor Coates's lips break into a grin that makes my blood turn to ice. The angrier and more passionate he gets, the thicker and more pronounced his British accent becomes. "But you didn't appreciate my work, did you? You didn't see what we could accomplish together."

"You're a monster!" I scream, my voice echoing through the room, and hopefully out into the night.

"A monster would have just killed you that first night. I'm not a monster, Blair. I'm a genius. I groomed you. I manipulated you to fall right into my lap without so much as a second thought. I was the puppet master to your little stringed body, and you still haven't stopped dancing for me."

He's right. I was like his puppet, and fell for the whole thing. The dream of working for someone like him had blinded me to what was really in front of me. A true monster. That day of my interview, I should've known it wasn't him trying to seduce me, or use my attack to further his research. It was him wanting to possess me. I fell for it hook, line, and sinker.

"Did you know it was your own advisor who put you in my crosshairs? The day I met with her to discuss my research, I saw you standing outside her office, putting up your little flyer. That red hair of yours trailing down your back to those skimpy shorts, begging for someone to fuck you."

His hands come toward me again, this time slipping into the waistband of my jeans. He moans as he gropes me. I can't stop myself from gagging.

"But to learn from your very own lips that you were a fan of my work? Well, that just made it all so much easier. I came to your house that night, not intending to hurt you, but to observe you. You piqued my interest, but I wanted to know if you could keep it. When I saw you there, alone, in your house, it was too perfect to walk away from. I had to taste you."

His hand slips out of my jeans, but doesn't leave my body. His palms migrate up to my shoulders, slip down over them, and squeeze my breasts.

"The way your face looked that night as you opened the door has been cemented into my mind ever since, tormenting me every time I closed my eyes. But I don't have to be tormented anymore. I have you now, and have you, I will."

He yanks back on the chair, and I go crashing to the

ground, the legs shattering upon impact. All the air rushes out of my lungs, and pain explodes with a snapping sound under my weight.

"Fuck!" I bellow. "My hand!"

"That's it," he coos. "I want to hear your pain."

He moves to his knees, trying to pry my feet apart while I fight against his strength. He's ready to finish his job, to take the one thing he hasn't gotten from me already.

My fear and terror take over, forcing my brain away from what's about to happen, immobilizing me from fighting back. My voice is gone. My body is rigid. Even the throbbing in my hands disappears. My entire system freezes. With nothing left, he's going to take what he wants, and I'm helpless to stop him.

He paws at my legs, trying to force them apart while I focus on the memory of GP's face inside my mind.

Pulling out a knife from his pocket, he rips and slices away my clothes, leaving me naked.

"Be a good girl and scream for me. I want to feel the last of your will to live leave you as I take your spirit."

He presses his groin against me, and I let out one final scream before my body plummets into darkness.

Forgive me, GP.

GREENPEACE

"WE'LL FIND HER, GP," Hashtag says, his words meant to soothe, me but all they do is piss me off.

"Yeah? How the fuck do you know? We've gone through almost every single building and found nothing. How do we even know she's here? We don't. We're going on a hunch."

Hashtag opens his mouth to answer, and that's when we hear it. A faint, high-pitched scream, filled with pain and terror. We move as one toward the sound, and I feel like my feet can't move fast enough. That was Blair, and she's hurt. She needs me to save her, and I just can't fucking move any faster.

"Over here," Hashtag calls out to a few others.

I forgo kicking the lock this time, and use my fist to break through the glass door.

Voices come closer, but I don't wait around. Rushing

inside, safety glass crunching under my boot, I hold my hand up to silence Hashtag. My ears strain. *Please, Blair, make another sound.* But she doesn't.

My heart thrashes in my ears, my chest tightens as my fear for her turns to desperation. And then a sound I will never get out of my head for as long as I live reaches my ears. The gleeful laugh of a man completely off his rocker floats around us, bouncing around the empty hallway in a ghostly echo.

"Basement," Hashtag says, but I'm already moving, scanning every door and sign for something that indicates the way to the basement. The heavy footsteps of my brothers echo at my back.

The basement stairs lie behind a heavy wooden door. This sign is so small, it's almost illegible in the darkness. One by one, we file through the door with me in the lead.

I pound down the stairs, not giving a shit if I alert the attacker at this point or not. I don't give a fuck, because this time, there's no escape. He's gotten past me before, but he won't get past my brothers.

The basement is empty, and mostly open, but for one lone door. It stands at the back of the room, and my best guess is that it leads to what could be the boiler room of the building. It's also where he's making my Blair scream in pain.

I dash across the open floor, and I don't even bother trying the knob. The time for civility is long past. I lift my foot and ram it beside the doorknob. Wood splinters and cracks before the door crashes open and slams against the wall.

What's inside sends me into a rage that pulls me from my mission of saving my girl, and forces me into one in which my only goal is to kill this man.

Blair's lying on the floor, a broken chair beneath her. She's not screaming anymore, because she's unconscious. Her eyes are swollen, her lip's split, and a terrifying amount of blood has pooled around her. Her pants have been shredded, leaving her exposed. And hovering above her, a look of annoyance and anger on his face, is an older man with a comb over.

"I'll fucking kill you!" I roar, snatching him up from his place between her legs.

"No!" he screams, his eyes bulging with rage. "No, you can't have her! She's mine! She was mine before you came along. You can't stop us from being together."

I don't know what the fuck he's talking about, and frankly, I don't give a shit. My boot connecting with his chin shuts him up pretty damn quick, and his crazy ranting is replaced by groans of pain.

"Please," he whines, pieces of his teeth spewing from his mouth with his plea.

"GP!" Karma calls. "Blair needs you."

Stone Face appears at my side. "Let me handle him. You go to your girl."

I look behind me, and when my eyes land on Blair once more, my heart shatters in my chest. Karma had taken off his T-shirt and draped it over her exposed body, and it's already soaked with blood.

"It's bad, man. She's cut up everywhere."

"Blair?" I call, crawling on my knees to get to her. "Baby? Baby, please wake up. Please wake up, Blair."

She doesn't move.

I feel helpless. I lift my gaze and peer up at Karma. "What are we gonna do? I can't lose her, Karma. I can't."

Karma's eyes drift around the room. His jaw hardens and his nostrils flare. "We're not gonna lose her, GP. No way in hell is this how it ends."

I stroke Blair's blood-soaked hair away from her face, speaking soft words of encouragement to her as Karma barks orders at the others behind me. I can't pay attention to anything he says, not right now. Right now, all I can do is be close to my girl, and pray this isn't the end for her. For us. *Please, God.*

Chapter 33

BLAIR

DEATH IS SO unlike what I thought it would be. There's no white light at the end of the tunnel. My grandmother didn't welcome me into a beautiful world of happiness. If anything, it's the polar opposite of everything I grew up learning about the afterlife. It's a sea of darkness. It's pain. There is no peace here.

"Blair," a voice calls out to me from the shadows. My ethereal being floats to find the sound, but nothing is there.

"Baby, wake up," it calls again. This time, the darkness shifts like a boat on the sea. A crack forms near the border around me, and light peeks through. My fingers trace it. I tap it, and the crack expands farther.

"Come back to me, Red."

GP! The crack expands even more, until a burst of light blinds me, and pain punches through my chest, making the darkness fall away. All that's left when I finally open my eyes is blinding light.

"Thank fuck," GP whispers, his handsome face coming into view.

His large body pulls at mine, embracing me tightly against him. The haze lifts from my vision, and an unfamiliar room comes into view.

"You've been out for three days. I thought I'd lost you." He nuzzles me tighter, like I'm going to float away.

A searing pain shoots through every part of my body, causing me to hiss, and he releases me instantly.

"Fuck. You okay?" His voice holds a nervous tenderness that I've never heard from him before. He's scared.

"It hurts," I whimper.

"I know, baby." Gently, he readjusts my pillow, and helps me settle on the bed.

The pain radiates through me as he tries to shift me back into a comfortable position.

"Better?"

I nod, noticing my hand in a white cast, all the way up to my elbow. I lift it, testing its unfamiliar weight.

"It's broken," he informs me. "The club has a doctor on retainer, and we took you to his clinic. You've got a concussion and some stab wounds. Luckily, nothing vital was hit. The doc stitched you up, and we've been taking care of you here, at the clubhouse…" He voice trails off, and his shoulders fall. "It's my fault he hurt you. I should never have left you behind."

"No," I argue, my voice a barely audible rasp.

He shoves off the bed, his weight roughly shifting the springs, making me bounce in pain. "He got to you because I left you unprotected. He did this…" His eyes fall to my body before he looks away. "I stopped him before he could…" He trails off again.

A weight lifts off of me. His darkest wish didn't come to fruition. My body would never be his.

"You saved me," I remind him, though I don't remember anything from the moment the chair hit the floor to waking up here. Whether or not it was the concussion, or my mind's way of sheltering me away from the worst of the memories, I would never know.

"We almost didn't, Red. After finding Lindsey in the hospital, I was sure we were too late. That I fucking lost you."

Did he say Lindsey? "She's alive?"

"Barely. But she's a fighter, just like you are. Judge is at the hospital with her now."

Hot, wet tears spill over and down my cheeks at the news. I could live with my death, but not hers. Knowing that we both made it makes my survival more meaningful. We both made it.

"Did you kill him?" My heart races at the thought that with his death, I would truly be free from the madness that my life has become. Free to feel safe again without praying he isn't standing around the corner, waiting to strike me down again.

"You were in bad shape when we got there. You were my priority."

"Is he...? He's still...?" *No, he can't be.* My throat tightens, and my chest heaves with anxiety. It's not possible.

"Yes," he replies coolly. "But not for long."

"He's here?"

"In the barn. Judge wanted to make sure you'd pull through before we decide what to do with him."

My heart races, nearly exploding at thought of him still alive, and so close to me. GP walks to me, sits on the edge of the bed, and takes my good hand in his, holding on to me like I'm a dream trying to slip away.

"I'm going to kill him, Blair, for everything he's done to you. His life is mine." His tone is laced with intent to fulfill his promise, and it scares me.

I've seen him angry before, but this is an entirely different level. This isn't anger. It's determination. It's retribution.

"I'll watch him bleed."

A soft knock comes from the door to the right of us, and Hashtag walks in with a stack of papers in his hands.

"Got something you both may want to see." He

hands over the papers. "There are tons of them. It took a lot of digging through missing persons reports, but he's linked to at least fourteen other disappearances, all women."

GP's eyes widen with each page he shuffles through in the stack. "Fuck, Hash. How'd he get away with this shit?"

"No idea, man. I've seen some fucked-up shit in my life, but this guy,"—tapping the professor's picture clipped to the top of the stack—"is at the top of the pile. Every university he's been affiliated with has a case. All redheads. All grad students."

"How did the police not connect the dots?"

"No bodies, man. Not one of them have been found."

"What about his wife?" I ask.

GP's head snaps to me.

"He kept talking about his wife."

"Page three," Hashtag answers. "Filed for divorce in the UK in 2000. No paper trail since then. It's like she's a ghost."

"She's dead. He told me he killed her."

Hashtag takes the pile from GP's hands. "Judge says it's up to you."

"Put a bullet in his head," GP responds.

"Not you," he clarifies.

Both of the men turn to look at me.

"It's her call."

It should be an easy one. He tried to kill me, he's killed others. *But am I strong enough to take his life?* Victims often say that justice being dealt to those who harmed them feels like a weight lifted off their shoulders. A second chance at a happy and peaceful life. I feel none of that. Absolutely nothing but fear of how I'll live with such a choice.

"I want to see him."

"Absolutely fucking not," GP bellows, pushing off the bed in a hurry. "I don't want you anywhere near him."

"It's my choice, isn't it?"

GP wants to argue with me. I can see it in his fiery eyes, but to deny me this would not only defy his club president's wishes, but it would also deny me my only chance at closure. I want to see his face one last time. To see the terror in his eyes. The same terror he put into mine. Only then can I affirm that justice will truly be done.

I try to shove my leg over the edge of the bed under my own power, but I'm too weak to stand. GP and Hashtag catch me before I fall off the bed completely.

"Take it easy there, young blood," Hashtag chuckles. "You're not up for running a marathon just yet. Let's try walking first."

Each of them take one of my arms, gently helping me to my feet. I test my strength, but I stumble at a single step. I try again. This time, I find a better footing. With both of them supporting me, they lead me out into the main space of the clubhouse. The last time I was here, it was so full of life. Now, it stands empty. Turning toward a door on the south end of the clubhouse, the shift makes me stumble again, and I lean all of my weight against GP.

"Fuck it." His large arms scoop me up and cradle me against his chest. The pain pings throughout my body like rapid fire, but he refuses to apologize this time. "I can't watch you struggle, Red. If you're hell-bent on doing this, I'm carrying you."

Hashtag leads the way and opens the door. Cold, southern night air hits me like a lightning bolt the moment we step outside. An old, weathered red barn sits in front of us. We move slowly toward it, and for a moment, I want to tell them to stop. To turn around. To help me forget that any of this ever happened.

Two large men stand guard outside of the door. "Why is she out here?" one of them asks. "She looks like shit."

"Watch it," GP growls. "It's her call. Judge's orders."

He nods, reaches over to the handle, and yanks open the large, heavy door. GP starts to carry me inside, but I stop him.

"Put me down," I demand.

"You can barely stand, Red."

"I want him to see me standing on my own two feet. I

want him to see he can't take my strength from me anymore."

He considers it for a few seconds before gently placing me back on my own feet. I double over, biting back my cry of pain.

You can do this, Blair. Use everything you've got. Don't show him how badly he's hurt you.

I dig deep, using all the strength I have to take the first step. Pain hits hard. I take a second, and then move one foot right after the other until I'm inside the barn. GP stays a safe distance behind me. Close enough that, if I stumble, he can catch me, but far enough away that Professor Coates can only see me.

In the center of the barren barn, I find him bound by a chain around his wrists, suspended from the exposed rafters. His face is barely recognizable. The club had taken their pieces of flesh in retribution. They'd made him suffer until a decision could be made. A decision that now lies in my hands.

I step closer, but GP reaches from behind me, tugging on my shirt. A silent order to not go any farther.

Professor Coates's bloody face peers down at me. His lips move, trying to speak, but nothing comes out.

I observe him silently, taking to memory the way the man who had tormented me for so long hangs helpless in front of me. His power was taken away from him, just as he had taken mine.

"Do you know what I see when I look at you, Professor?" I say, my low voice echoing throughout the empty barn. "A weak man. A monster. You tried to take everything from me. You've already taken away from so many others. But not anymore. I'm taking back our power. For myself. For your wife. For all the other women you've hurt. It's over. You're not going to hurt anyone else."

He gurgles as he tries to speak, blood spilling from his lips.

"I *will* be your last victim."

Without so much as a second glance, I turn and walk away from the man whose name will be struck from the record books by me. By these men who have done so much to protect me. The last of my energy and strength leaves as I get out of his sight. GP swoops in and carries me back out of the barn.

"Do it," I tell him, without an ounce of hesitation. "Finish this."

Chapter 34

GREENPEACE

"BET YOU THOUGHT you'd broken her," I spit through clenched teeth as I drag his own blade down his bare torso, slitting his belt in two. "You didn't, though, did you? You saw that for yourself. Blair Thompson is stronger than you ever were."

"Please," he sobs, his head shaking from side to side. "Please don't do this. I'll stop. I'll leave Blair alone. You can have her."

His words tip my anger over the edge.

"She was already mine!" I scream into his old, sweaty face, causing him to sob even harder, his entire body trembling with fear and anguish. "She's mine because she fucking wants to be, not because I made her, you psycho fuck."

Using my knife, I slice his pants the way he sliced

Blair's, and when I'm done, he hangs before me, completely naked. His shoulders quiver with his tears, his wails drowning out every other noise. "Just get it over with," he wails.

"Not so fast, Professor," I say with a smile. "We have a little game we want to play first."

Hashtag approaches, the stack of reports on Coates's victims in his hands. Handing me the stack, I pass the blade to an excited looking Stone Face.

"You know what this is?" I ask, waving the papers in the air. Coates doesn't answer. He just continues to cry, but I know he can still hear me. "This is a printout of every single one of your crimes. Each page, another woman you hurt."

His tears grow quiet, and he lifts his head to watch me.

"That's right, Professor. You've been found out. You've got victims all over the world, and they want to play the game too."

His brow furrows, and his trembles turn to full-on shakes.

Stone Face steps in front of him and spins the blade around and around. "Wanna hear how we play?"

Coates shakes his head wildly, but Stone Face is in his element.

"GP here is going to read out the names of each one

of your innocent victims." Stone Face raises the knife higher so Coates can see it. "For each name, I get to pick a place to shove this into your body. One stab per name. But don't worry. I'll draw it out so each girl gets her turn."

"No!" he cries again, this time slumping in defeat. "I'm sorry. I'm so very sorry."

Stone Face looks me in the eye and nods.

"Vanessa Riggins," I read out, then drop her page to the floor.

Stone Face scans Coates up and down, then drives the blade deep into the side of his belly. Coates screams, over and over, wailing and flailing, praying to a God that surely must have forsaken him before.

When he's silent, I read the next name. "Gwyn Ackerman."

Stone Face plunges again. Coates screams and cries and prays, and when it's quiet, I read the next name. Stone Face stabs him again. The game continues—every stab a crude memorial for each woman unfortunate enough to cross his path and dare to have red hair.

After I've read the last page, Coates is sagging from his chain. The other guys from the club are all here, leaning against the side of the barn, taking in this sick punishment. Coates looks worn, bloodless, and on the brink of death.

"There's one more name," Judge calls from the side."

I glance over as he steps forward.

"Take the blade, GP," he orders.

I do as I'm told.

"Those other women are the victims you've killed," Judge tells Coates. "But there are two women you couldn't." He narrows his eyes, growling out the name, "Lindsey Sheridan."

Lindsey had been hurt protecting Blair. I sink the blade deep into the professor's belly.

Judge waits until I pull it clear, and for the professor to stop his shrieking. Once Coates is quiet enough to hear him, Judge scowls. "And finally, this last one is for Blair Thompson."

When I hear her name, I picture her the way I had found her twice now because of this man. Broken, bloody, on the brink of death. All because he has some sick thing for red hair. Roaring with rage, I pull my arm back and bring the knife down, into Coates's heart.

His mouth gapes open in shock, his eyes locked on mine while his body shakes and jerks in its bindings. I watch the light of life evaporate from his evil eyes, feeling numb that I killed a man, but proud to tell my girl I slayed her dragon.

Once he's gone, I drop the knife to the floor and stare at nothing.

"You did the right thing, GP," Judge insists, clapping his hand down on my shoulder. "I'm so fucking proud of you."

"Even though I lied," I joke, my heart only half in it.

"Especially because you lied. I'm a dickhead some-times. And every once in a while, dickheads need a reminder about what exactly they stand for."

I grin back at him, feeling his approval like a son would revel in the approval of his own father.

"Go be with your girl," he orders.

I don't make him tell me twice. I step over the mess of bloody hay on the floor and head out of the barn, accepting back slaps and congratulations from the rest of the guys.

When I step into the room I keep here at the club-house, the shower is running. I can hear Blair's sobs, and each one rips a slice through my heart. That poor woman has been through more in the past few weeks than most people go through in a lifetime.

"Baby," I call, stepping into the bathroom. "You doing okay?"

She sniffs and clears her throat on the other side of the curtain. "Yeah," she answers, her voice filled with sadness.

With the tip of my finger, I slide back the edge of the curtain and find her on the floor of the tub, her arms wrapped around her knees, her hair soaked and matted to her head, her tears mixing with the fall of shower water.

"Oh, Red," I say, kicking off my shoes. "Don't cry, baby. It's over now."

She nods, not looking up at me, and wipes her red nose on her arm. "I know. I know it is. I'm trying, GP. I'm really trying."

Not bothering to remove my clothes, I step over the edge of the tub and into the shower. Adjusting her battered, stitched up body, I fold myself into the space behind her, pulling her into my arms.

"I'm so sorry," she sobs, her body trembling.

I frown, pulling her closer. "What on Earth are you sorry for?"

"I'm sorry I brought this to you. I'm sorry I didn't see it sooner. I'm sorry I got you caught up in this shit."

I can't help but smirk. Pulling my head back, I lift her body away from mine and turn her around to face me, so I can meet her gaze. "Red, if none of this had happened, I wouldn't have you. Don't you ever be sorry for something you can't control. And definitely don't be sorry for being in my life, because I wouldn't want it any other way."

She looks away from me. "I'm broken, GP. He broke me."

I force her to look at me again, giving her a little shake. "What happened to that spitfire I just saw in the barn earlier? The one that wanted to prove to Coates he didn't break her?"

"I'm not her," she sobs. "That was a lie."

"That's bullshit, and you know it, Red."

"GP, the person I used to be ceased to exist the night he attacked me. The person he left behind is unrecognizable to me. Someone you pity, not someone you love. I'm the priceless family heirloom that no one wants to hold for fear of it shattering in their hands."

"I'm in love with you, Blair," I blurt out. "Have been since the day you tried to force me into playing house when we were kids. Nothing will ever change that. Not even your own self-doubt."

"You shouldn't love me," she cries. "I'm a mess."

"You're my mess, Red. I killed the man who hurt you. I'd do it again a million times over if it meant you're still here with me. And I want you here with me. Just you and me."

The sadness on her face fades a little. "And Walter and Jinx?" she adds.

I curl my nose. "Well... Walter for sure."

The sadness fades a little more, and a smile spreads across her face. "You love Jinx and you know it."

"Jinx is an asshole."

Then, she gifts me with the most beautiful sound I've ever heard in my life. She throws her head back and laughs. She laughs long and hard, and when she finishes, she presses her face against my sopping wet T-shirt covered chest. "I love you too, GP."

BLAIR

IN THE NEARLY TWO weeks that have passed since I made the decision to end the professor's life, I've sat in silent contemplation countless times, trying to reconcile that morally, I should be appalled about ordering a man to die. A monster put out to pasture by my own boyfriend's hand. GP refused to tell me what he did to him, but seeing the professor's face plastered all over the local and national news was more than enough for me. How the club had managed to implicate him in all the other horrendous murders he'd committed was the bow on the gift. That's what they gave me. Their unacknowledged addition would help so many families find closure that I now have.

They rallied around me like family, and trusted me to do the right thing.

"I've been thinking," I inform GP, who's flipping burgers on the grill outside the clubhouse.

"About letting the prospect finish the grilling and we head to my room?"

I roll my eyes, and he laughs.

"Didn't you get enough of me earlier?"

He'd been insatiable since the club's doctor gave me a clean bill of health. My hand was healing nicely, and the stab wounds looked great. They'd scar, but I didn't care about that. Those scars were badges of courage, to remind me of what I'd been through. What I had survived.

"I'll never be able to get enough of you, Red. Not even when we're old. My wrinkly ass will still be trying to get into your pants."

"That is not an image I want to think about, asshole," Judge chimes in with a look of disgust on his face. "Darling, if you ever get tired of this guy, you just give me a call. I'll take care of him for you." He throws a wink at me for good measure.

"The fuck you will, prez. She's my girl." He stares back at him, pointing the spatula at his head. "I can still whip your big ass."

"I got a twenty on that if you throw down here and now," Karma laughs, whipping out a bill from his wallet and throwing it to the ground.

"I don't want to embarrass you in front of your girl.

About done flipping the meat?"

GP flips him the middle finger instead. Judge, and a few of the guys, head back inside, leaving us alone again. I catch Judge motioning to GP out of the corner of my eye. I start to ask him what's going on, but he circles back to our earlier conversation.

"You going to tell me or leave me in suspense before those assholes interrupt us again?"

"I was thinking about my house."

"Oh?" He arches his brow.

The last few days, we've been talking about our housing issue. He, of course, wanted me to put my house on the market and move in with him. Not like we weren't living together already, but his point is what got me thinking. Grandmother's house had always been my home. A place of comfort. After the attack, its memories were stolen from me, but it didn't have to be that way. It could be a home that brought hope and love again.

"I don't want to sell it. I want to convert it to a recovery house for battered women."

His brows rise in surprise. "Wow. Not what I expected you to say."

"I've been doing a little research. There are all these different kinds of women's shelters around town, but none of them are for domestic violence."

"I can tell there's more going on in that head of yours." He flips the burgers, and they sizzle. Satisfied, he closes the lid and comes to sit by me in the extra patio chair Priest had drug out for me.

"I sent an email to Professor McCallen last night. She wants to volunteer as a counselor. This could really work. It can serve an unmet need, and maybe it would be a good avenue for me after I graduate. There's a lot I'd have to do to get the permits and the 503c status to fundraise, but I want to give it a shot."

"The smile on your face tells me all I need to know. If that's want you want to do, Red, I'm all in with you."

I lean toward him, wrapping my arms around his shoulders. "There's just one little problem." I smile up at him. "I'll need a place to stay."

He laughs. "You asking to move in, Red?" repeating back the very same thing I'd teased him about the morning he made me breakfast.

"I mean, I'd have to ask my boyfriend if he would be okay with it…" His lips crash onto mine, cutting off my words, and I kiss him back just as hard.

"There's one thing we have to do first before I agree to all this." He shoves out of the chair and reaches his hand down to me. I take it. "Follow me, Red."

With a skeptical look, I do as he says, following him straight into the clubhouse where the entire club stands in a semi-circle around the door. All eyes are on me, making me really uneasy. He squeezes my hand reassuringly.

"What's going on?"

"Here's the thing, Red. That night I claimed you, I forget about something."

"Okay…"

GP releases my hand and walks to where his club stands. Judge hands him something, claps his hand on GP's shoulder, and nods. GP swivels and moves methodically back to me.

"Claiming you was the best damn thing I've ever done, but I know I didn't give you a choice in the matter." Looking back to his brothers over his shoulder, he continues. "This club is a brotherhood. A family. We live, ride, and die, side by side. We protect our family, and I'd like you to be a part of it."

"But I thought I already was?"

"Then I guess this makes the next part easier."

He brings the object Judge gave him out in front of him. A smaller version of his own cut. He unfolds it, revealing my property patch on the back of it, with his name stitched in underneath it. He turns it again to show me the front, and on the upper right-hand breast is my name embroidered onto a patch.

I beam, tracing my name with my fingertip.

"You saying yes?"

"I've always wanted a family."

"I need to hear you say the words, Red."

"Hell yes!" I squeal. "Now, are you going to put that

on me, or do I need to do that myself?"

He pops open the buttons and holds it out for me to slip it over my shoulders. I try to adjust the stiff leather with my good hand. GP leans in close with the pretense of helping me, but his face tells a different story. "When we get home tonight, I want to see you wearing this, and only this."

The promise of our own celebration to come later makes me shiver. I turn to face the club, seeing pride clear as day on all their faces.

"Welcome home, Red."

Home never felt so good.

HASHTAG

It's nights like this that make me appreciate that I'm not tied down like some of these fuckers. Just watching them parade around with the big ass grins on their faces is enough to make me uneasy. I tried the whole relationship thing once—the bitch fucking broke me. Nobody's gonna get a chance to pull that shit with me again.

Priest plops down next to me at the bar, ordering a drink from one of the club girls who's tending for tonight's festivities. She pops the lid and slides the bottle over to him.

"Great party," he declares, taking a pull from his beer as he leans back against the bar. "She's good for him. For all of us."

I can only nod in response. Yeah, it worked out for him. Blair's good people. I like her. But sitting here watching the two of them celebrate their love is not going so well for me tonight. It's not Blair or GP. It's not the other people crowding the clubhouse and having a good time. It's the date. Our date. What would have been our wedding date.

"What's up your ass?"

"Nothing," I growl. "Just trying to drink my beer without you ladies spoiling it for me."

Priest glances over at me and shakes his head. "You're not happy for them, are you?"

"Didn't say I wasn't."

Priest takes another swig before slamming down the bottle onto the bar, tossing up his fingers to order another one. One of the club girls saunters over to me with her tits falling out of her top. Pressing them up against me, I shove her off.

"Not in the mood, sweetheart."

Her painted face saddens at my dismissal. It's nothing against her or that beautiful body of hers. If it were a different day, I'd be driving my cock into her, forgetting about all the bullshit.

"I don't get you, man. All these women around here, and I haven't seen you touch a single one of them lately."

"Hey, I got a question for you."

"What's that?"

"Does this barstool look like a fucking confessional, prospect?"

Without another word, Priest stalks off. Mission accomplished. Tonight's just the kind of night I want to sit here at this bar and get drunk. I shouldn't even be here. I'm in no mood for celebrating.

"Hot damn!" Karma yells out from the crowd.

Great. One of the club girls must be putting on a show. Grabbing my beer, I start to turn around when...

Fuck.

A fucking ghost from my past. One I never expected to walk back into his place so long as my lungs still sucked in air.

"Is he here?" her voice calls out over the noise, rocking my fucking world. The beer drops from my hand, shattering to the floor. She turns her gaze upon me, zeroing in.

Fuck me sideways. Ain't no hiding from her now. *Way to go, asshole.*

She bolts toward me, fear clear as day on that pretty face I used to call mine all those years ago. The face that fucking bailed without so much as a goddamn word.

The years have been good to her. Damn good. The

girl I knew has grown into a woman, and a smoking hot one at that. Every pair of unattached male eyes are on her. The beast lying dormant inside of me growls, wanting to re-stake my claim on her, and force them to look away. But she's not mine anymore. She'd made that clear enough when she left.

"Hash," her silky voice calls out to me.

"So, you do remember my name. Wasn't sure you would the way you left."

Her beautiful blue eyes soften as a tear slides down her cheek.

"I need your help."

"I ain't in the helping mood, darling. Not anymore. Go ask someone else," I snarl, stepping around her.

"Please," she pleads. "Someone's taken my daughter."

So she has a kid. That fact hits me like a sucker punch to the gut.

I don't turn to look at her when I ask from over my shoulder, "And why should I care about some other man's spawn?"

"Because she's yours, Hash."

———

Read more about Hashtag's story in Dark Secret.

THE SERIES

Dark Protector

Dark Secret

Dark Guardian

Dark Desires

Dark Destiny

Dark Redemption

Dark Salvation

Dark Seduction

Avelyn Paige is a USA Today and Wall Street Journal bestselling author who writes stories about dirty alpha males and the brave women who love them. She resides in a small town in Indiana with her husband and three fuzzy kids, Jezebel, Cleo, and Asa.

Avelyn spends her days working as a cancer research scientist and her nights sipping moonshine while writing. You can often find her curled up with a good book surrounded by her pets or watching one of her favorite superhero movies for the billionth time. Deadpool is currently her favorite.

ALSO BY AVELYN PAIGE

The Heaven's Rejects MC Series

Heaven Sent

Angels and Ashes

Sins of the Father

Absolution

Lies and Illusions

The Dirty Bitches MC Series

Dirty Bitches MC #1

Dirty Bitches MC #2

Dirty Bitches MC #3

Other Books by Avelyn Paige

Girl in a Country Song

Cassie's Court

Geri Glenn writes alpha males. She is a USA Today Bestselling Author, best known for writing motorcycle romance, including the Kings of Korruption MC series. She lives in the Thousand Islands with her two young girls, one big dog and one terrier that thinks he's a Doberman,, a hamster and two guinea pigs whose names she can never remember.

Before she began writing contemporary romance, Geri worked at several different occupations. She's been a pharmacy assistant, a 911 dispatcher, and a caregiver in a nursing home. She can say without a doubt though, that her favorite job is the one she does now—writing romance that leaves an impact.

ALSO BY GERI GLENN

The Kings of Korruption MC series.

Ryker

Tease

Daniel

Jase

Reaper

Bosco

Korrupted Novellas:

Corrupted Angels

Reinventing Holly

Other Books by Geri Glenn

Dirty Deeds (Satan's Wrath MC)

Hood Rat

Made in United States
Troutdale, OR
07/18/2023

11391795R00166